An Adventure

REAL

LIFE OF THOR

by
Joel Forrester

Cover Artwork
THOR'S BATTLE AGAINST THE JÖTNAR
by Mårten Eskil Winge (1872)

Evergreen Books
New York - 2016

FOR MARY

ÜBER EDITOR: TONY BLY

Cover Artwork
THOR'S BATTLE AGAINST THE JÖTNAR
by Mårten Eskil Winge (1872)

Additional Artwork
Lorenz Frølich (1820-1908)

MUSIC PAGES

Go to:

www.joelforrester.com

to hear these selections

"THOR, HAVING TROUBLE GETTING DIFFERENTIATED"
(See Chapter 27)
by Lorenz Frølich (1820-1908)

GODS IMAGINED (Prelude)

6

(1)

SCHNORRI (audio only): *Zzzzz! Zzzzz! Zzzzz!*

(2)

What is a God, imagined? He must vastly surpass me in some known aspect; yet the aspect itself we must hold in common or my lifeline to this stellar being is broken and himself left unimaginable: raggedly Modern, dependent on belief. And, beyond that aspect, other elements of his character must lie within the recognizably un-Godlike. Norse Thor fits the pattern to a T. He never loses heart---as I will, time to time---but he is no brighter than I am. His actions flow ever from his persona: that is the true mark of the Divine. Whereas, the final third of my life has brought me no closer to Thor's sacred integrity: I'm still all over the place. ...But his doings fall into narrative, seek the inevitability of melody; and so do mine.

Gods don't age; they inhabit Wittgenstein's Eternity, the Present. But they know they won't live forever. Thor and all the other Aesir have been aware, since the first bloom of consciousness, that they were fated each to die in an apocalyptic battle named Rognarok and that their opponents would be the Mountain Giants and the Frost Giants, whose ranks would be swelled by various monsters, physical and ghostly. Aware also that existence would survive this battle but in a world without Gods or Giants, ours.

(3)

Thor was bothered. His lumbering thoughts could not resolve the difficulty, no matter how hard he shook his head, no matter how frighteningly he threatened his own brain. 'How is it possible?' he asked himself repeatedly. 'How can one with as stout a heart as mine even *imagine* defeat, let alone death? No force I have ever come up against has proved anywhere near that lethal! Nowhere near.' And yet he knew there was a power that lay beyond his: one, unlike his, utterly unfettered by Time, one that spoke in terms of inevitability; and that this power was summarized by those weird sisters, the Norns; and that the Norns had assured him of his eventual death.

After much spinning of his cogitative wheels, the huge dude from Donnerstag concluded that he *couldn't* know about what he *didn't* know about; we might say that Thor's problem was one of "experience" or the lack thereof. Adventures had he had aplenty but the setting was always either Asgard (where the Gods pitched their houses) or, crossing the Rainbow Bridge, Midgard (where the humans lived). One-on-one, his own size dwarfed that of humanity's stoutest, he knew that; but he had never actually *seen* a Giant, so was left incapable of taking the measure of this agent of his ultimate undoing.

And so, in time, Thor came to reckon that---although in terms of courage he was first among equals in Asgard and a literal God to the humans---it was incumbent on him to journey to a place where he might well find himself diminished. Yes, he must go to Jotenheim and size up these Giants, even if it bring the last day nearer. Especially then: as a being beyond fear itself, Thor definitely had no fear of the truth.

But many of his adventures to date---although displaying Thor's hallmark courage and the winning brutality with which he wielded his famous hammer (which struck with unerring accuracy any target its holder held in mind; and returned forthwith to his hand)---nonetheless also tended to manifest the God's slow-moving thought processes.   Latterly, Thor had become aware of this, himself, and it presented him a second problem: Would he, in fact, know the truth if he saw it?

No, there was nothing for it but that he invite Loki to accompany him on this quest. Loki was, by a long chalk, the cleverest of the Immortals. Odin was the *deepest* thinker in Asgard, but His knowledge---gained at the expense of one eye by drinking from the well that nourishes the tree in which all the worlds are hung---was apparently of the undifferentiated/cosmic variety, not the sort to be brought to bear on mundane or even extra-mundane problems. Was perspective beyond Him?, part 'n' parcel of His perceptual sacrifice? ...But in any case, Odin was the Unmoved Mover; one couldn't just sign Him up for a jolly God-jaunt! Loki, on the other hand, knew hawks from handsaws and was himself half-Giant...although his comely features and ordinary quasi-human stature gave no clue what his father and his kin might look like. 'No,' Thor reasoned, 'the Giant in Loki comes out in his duplicity. No one is really sure of the Trickster's ultimate loyalty to Asgard. He seems to put "home" and "heart" in separate categories. Yet there is no doubt that he can think rings around me.' Thor sighed, all duality forever beyond his ken.   As with virtually every right-wing bully-boy, he was parlous mistrustful of any display of intelligence. But since his brave heart never permitted mistrust to shade into fear, Thor, the moment his head cleared, proceeded to call upon the Trickster.

* * *

[Picture these characters as you please; this is something in the way of being an improbably-lengthy radio play ... before an assembled audience?---JF]

THOR: I'm bound for Jotunheim, Loki.

LOKI: To get a foretaste of what the future would have you swallow?

THOR: I wouldn't put it that way....

LOKI: Thor, me lad, you couldn't disguise a purpose if you had the power to change your form! Which you don't, by the way. More in *my* line. [Smiles with malice; preens]

THOR: I'd never be other than I am.

LOKI: We all have problems. ...By the way: yes, I'll accompany you on this fool's errand.

THOR: How could---?

LOKI: ---I have divined what you "had in mind"?, if I may indulge in overstatement. Quite simple. Quite as simple as thou, Hammerhead. You would not have told me of this expedition had you not required my involvement. You'd consider it none of my business, were it *not* my business. Get it?

THOR: I could have been merely passing the time in converse with thee, Trickster. Or I could have been seeking thy advice, half-breed that you are.

LOKI: Are there any recorded instances of your doing the like? Or anything like the like? Hmmm? You don't even know whether to be familiar or formal with me! [Reflectively:] Nor I with thee.

THOR (grimly): We set out at dawn.

LOKI (claps his hands with glee): That's more like it! Lay down the law!! Leave speculation to those with an appreciation of spectacle. ...Now I must go gorge myself; I've a presage that I shan't be permitted free indulgence of my prodigious appetites on this would-be reconnaissance mission of yours.

THOR: You will never learn, Trickster, that there is strength in the control of appetite.

LOKI: Nor will it ever penetrate your Divine Density that other beings are not just inaccurate versions of yourself. Although---I admit it!---there is power in that: strength through ignorance, yes! ...Whereas, *my* strength lies in a sublime willingness to *scratch every itch.*

THOR: Though you disgust me, yet I find I need you.

LOKI: Well-spoken, Thick-o! Until the morrow, then.

(4)

It was the morning of Odin's Day, Odin the All-in-All, Ontology. Your Wednesday, Reader.

Our two ill-sorted comrades took off at dawn, as planned. But this constituted the whole of Thor's planning. He'd failed even to pack provisions, so great was his belief in the tendency of events to shape themselves around his needs and desires: indeed, he'd had no other experience of life but this, so we cannot in conscience blame him, can we?

Loki, of course, toted a full mess kid and plenty of mess. He'd also urged Thor to bring his (Thor's) two sacred goats as pack animals; these were regenerative beings, if properly propitiated, and the Thunderer had to admit that they might come in handy. (Laboring, Thor's mind twisted this admission into a contorted hymn of self-praise: 'Yes! I was *correct* to have brought Loki along!', as if the future contained an outline that only needed to be matched up with! ...Are children still gifted with paint-by-number sets?)

Thor's self-belief had also predictably constrained him from considering matters such as distance or direction. And Loki was, as was usual with him, just along for the ride. Little wonder, then, that the journey proved far, far longer than either had anticipated. They'd crossed the Rainbow Bridge into Midgard easily enough but the whole of Midgard had to be traversed before they reached Jotenheim and Midgard seemed to scroll on forever!

"Whoever would have thought," Thor mused aloud as they trudged along, day and night losing strict form, "that the humans ---puny and weak as they are---could inhabit such a huge world!"

"Okey-doke! And this, my Unseen Audience, is what passes for lofty thought in that dullard brain of his," Loki declared. "And, by the way, Thor?: between the two of us, we've eaten up nearly all the grub I packed."

With that the two fell silent. Humanity had begun radically to thin out. Perhaps that meant our boys were, at last, nearing Jotenheim. An hour passed during which they saw no human habitation. Hunger began to attack them; Thor welcomed it as a test of his discipline; Loki embraced it as a primal wellspring of gallows humor, his verbal specialty. "Keep your demise clearly in mind," the Trickster forever told self and others: "It is the hidden source of all vitality! No life without death!!" *And yet...*both these Deities, each against his character, began to be hard on each other as hunger ate away at what were, after all, mere principles. Also, the temperature had taken a bleeding nosedive.

And so it was with profound relief that they greeted the arching, sulphurous plume of, presumably, a sod- or peat-fire, far off on the horizon. It took the two yet another passel of hours, even with their prodigious strides, to reach the origin of the plume. And, to the extent that a God may ever be truly disappointed, both Thor and Loki felt something of the sort (so characteristically human!) when they got close enough to see how subfusc, how very small and slovenly!, was the hovel that housed the fire, its smoke dwarfing the source.

"How do humans *live* this way?" Thor asked, whilst tying up his goats.

"Ho-ho! A rhetorical question!!" Loki mock-marveled. "What next?"

(5)

Thor forbore to boot in the door; he understood that humans were pure creatures of fear. And indeed when his lordly knock succeeded in throwing open the door *anyway*, he and Loki beheld a quaked-out family of four, backed all the way up to the fire, their hovel largely devoid of possessions of any sort, necessary or decorative.

A one-sided introduction did little to quell the quivering; and so Thor made, ham-handedly, to be gentle: "You needn't fear us," he said. "We come seeking shelter, a place to snooze, and food. That's all."

The man of the house tried to answer but his chattering teeth would not permit words to form. His wife stepped forward: "We don't fear you, formidable though you appear. No, **we're cold!!**"

LOKI: Ah!

WIFE: We've burned up nearly all our furniture...to keep from freezing to death. As to food, well, you're welcome to the thin gruel we've subsisted on for weeks now. We've nought else.

THOR (implacable): Understand, please, that we've no great sympathy for you. As Gods we are, at root, forces of Nature and, as such, self-protective and indifferent.

LOKI (explanatory): Thunderation here wouldn't know an "other" if it raised him to orgasm!

THOR (to Loki and to himself): Which I can generally achieve on my own.

LOKI (aside): And that thar is about as reflective as the dude gets, Folks!

THOR (to the quiverers): But I can promise you that we shall all eat well tonight. And, if you'll excuse me, I'll see to that now.

So saying, Thor stepped back outside and proceeded to build his own fire. The God then untethered his two goats and ritualistically slaughtered them (in sacrifice to himself, of course), vocally accompanying this bloody act with "a sort of runic rhyme", as Edgar A. might have voiced the play-by- play (before Baudelaire bettered him).

After he brought the heaped 'n' steaming goat-meat back inside, setting it on the floor (the table having been burnt just yesterday, it was explained), Thor delivered a brief, non-Dramatic homily: "Please don't thank me! We Gods find human gratitude emotionally intolerable. What I *shall* require is your obedience. Listen to me. You may eat heartily of the meat of these bones. But as each bone is picked clean, it must be taken outside and tossed into the fire I have made there. Yes?"

The family and Loki slathered their assent. Then all fell on the meat with a vengeance.

[We observers avert our faces until they have finished, Joyce having described the scene for all time in his Lestrygonian chapter; although the wedding banquet in Von Stroheim's GREED will get you there too.]

* * *

Teen-age is, as you may have read, a Modern social construct; if so, it were blatant projection on my part to ascribe the rebelliousness of the family-son to his pre-imago state. Indeed, Schnorri---the purblind Homer of Iceland---tells us the lad was helplessly conditioned to *waste nothing* (Weber in the wings) and that *that* was why, when he took his bone outside, he cracked it open and sucked out the marrow before chucking the sucker onto the fire: Was he not a credit to his conditioning?! And numberless children, hearing this corner of the story, have alternatively assumed that the boy was simply *still hungry* (yet another projection?); and if indeed the lad Thialfi had motive, means, and opportunity, he must nonetheless have considered what he did a victimless crime. If so, how wrong he was!

[Pause for reflection]

The exhausted Gods would sleep well enough, that night, having demanded something of a non-sexual *droit de seigneur* arrangement. Well, yes, the Trickster *had* considered a more literal application but the problem was: neither the human mother nor the father was anywhere near *attractive* enough. That left the children, a boy and girl. But Loki found his master-appetite, just then, was for a solid sleep. So he failed to demur when Thor booted the human family out of its one remaining piece of unburnt furniture, the bed. Oh, the Trickster had half a yen to pull the kids to him---with sleep the main course, they'd provide an intriguing *aperitif*---but, blissfully for our Midgardian sensibilities, the God conked out in mid-thought.

Yes; Dad, Mom, and the kids all slept on the floor. This is not an antique Greek tale of mortals being raised to the Heavens for showing hospitality to Gods traveling incognito. No; it is instead the more usual tale of powerful beings throwing their weight around. The weaker must needs accommodate and Mom, in admirable practicality, reminded her maternal brood that not only did they owe their full bellies to these overmastering strangers but that the floor would be their bed soon enough, wouldn't it?, so let's get used to it.

(6)

Practicality can answer many a hardship; but not even this noble wife and mother could withstand the wrath of a God.

Our sublime protagonists had been awake betimes---up, again, at the crack, in fact---and Thor had straightaway set about to pull off the regeneration ritual. The words are lost, of course [the old Schnoozer can't *guess* 'em into being], but they took immediate effect and, *mirabile dictu*, out of the ashes of the cold fire sprang the two goats! Until one fell over.

"What's this?!?" Thor bellowed. "What the fuck is this?" ...For one of the goats was undeniably lame. "Who fucked up the ritual??"

But, of course, he knew. Someone from this weak-willed humanite family had refused to follow orders; they, whose portion ought to have been pure gratitude, had instead disobeyed. Had disobeyed *him*, a God. Thor's rage was titanic, his vengeance would be immediate: screaming, he declared his firm intent to slaughter all within the house. He'd start with that silent, palsied father, rip out his prominent adam's apple. ...In truth, Thor had become the prototype "berserker": bloodlust personified, sheathed in a bear-skin. Loki just stood around and laughed merrily to himself.

* * *

From today's vantage, after 20 centuries influenced, to some extent, by the mercy of the Nazarene, all this seems brutal, ugly, and wrong. But I hold it important to see these high beings as they may actually have been conceived, answering and answerable to a long-buried corpus of human needs, speaking today (perhaps?) to inadmissible desires. A God had been offended through disobedience and so---as with Jehovah but never Jesus---bloody punishment had perforce to be inflicted, we are left to suppose....

THOR (wroth): "We"?? Yes and who the fuck are *you?*, singular?, plural? ...Trickster---whose voice is that?, that I'm hearing in my head?

LOKI (loath): Um.

NARRATOR (aka, Joel Forrester; with discomfort): I? I'm your Narrator.

THOR (furious): In a pig's ass you are! In a horse's eye!! I and I alone am the author of my words and deeds! Necessity alone is my master/mistress. You? You are a gnat buzzing in my brain.

LOKI (placatory): Sorry, Forrester. I know this must be disturbing for you. The "fictional character conscious of itself" has cut a trite 'n' tiresome figger...ever since Prospero drowned his book: I know! But Chief Thunderthud and I---as you've imagined us---*are* transcendental beings, you know. I, for one, inhabit many, many worlds simultaneously, although it feels like I bounce from branch to branch. And himself, here, got so het up---just being himself!---that he succeeded in rupturing your Reality Barrier. Be cool, though; Thor can't actually lay hands on you. As you are only a voice to him, he is only a voice to you. He and I and you: we're all voices: a mutual ventriloquism: a poison, if you will, poured homeopathically into the porches of your Reader's inmost ear. [To the Reader:] "Art thou there, Truepenny?"

THOR: And who the fuck's this "Jesus"? He one of them birds who'll line up with the Giants, come Rognarok?

LOKI (with barely-suppressed mirth): Ho-ho, no, Thor. Jesus?: he'd be one of those Humanist Gods, prominent in the next chapturn; you know, like Lao Tse and Kung. ...But then, of course, you wouldn't know, Thor: you can't read!

THOR (athunder): Life isn't a species of reflection!!!

NARRATOR (to Loki): How do I shut him up?, and you too, for that matter? [Shudders] ...And *me*, as well?

LOKI (shrugs): Just get on with the story. I'll handle the breech here. ...I'm an exhibitionist, of course, so I delight in the exposure. But I understand how the likes of you might quail at all the glare. And if you ever really came to identify with my big buddy here, you'd be *doing* things rather than writing about them, wouldn't you? ...Yes, I'll tidy up. But as your leading protag told that quartet of minor characters: keep any gratitude strictly unvoiced. Oh, Thursday nailed that one, I must admit; we Gods have trouble stomaching human sympathy in *any* form. Gives us **nausea**.

THOR: Trickster, I don't get it! You're carrying on a confab with the personified buzzing in *my* head?!?

LOKI (not without affection): Hush, Brother. Don't let it tax you. You'll notice that your rage has started to evaporate.

THOR (conceding the point): Well...yeah, I got distracted.

And it was true. There is much scholarly disagreement as to precisely why Thor failed to follow his nature and lay waste to the human household. Was the God indeed put through a change? "Distraction" is altogether too Modern a cause. Some have even conjured the descent (from the Western future?) of a proto-Galilean state of Grace. (Would you have Mom's practical bravery rewarded with punishment?) But I imagine it can be ascribed simply to the dictates of the story itself...or that's my working theory: the momentary shambles brought to a formerly firm fictional context providing a necessary emotional deflation, a subsiding. That satisfies *this* fabulist: a mere plot mechanism, nothing more. A blotted copybook.

[Loki---bestriding his own world and ours like a colossus--- coughed politely.]

In any case, for us late-Moderns, it's every whit as odd, as archaic, that it was somehow *perfectly acceptable* to Mom and Dad that their kids---in propitiation for Thialfi's disobedience--- be handed over to Thor and Loki as bond-servants! Schnorri even says, "And so they would remain 'til the end of Time," which sounds to me like "And that's why kangaroos have pouches, Boys 'n' Girls!", but let it pass.

LOKI (re-coughs): On with the story?

NARRATOR (immediately chastened): Yes. Sorry. Let me sow some stars and then I'll resume the narrative.

* * *

(7)

SCHNORRI: *Zzzz! Zzzz!*

(8)

So it was (however it was) that the two Deities set out again for Jotenheim, accompanied now by the lad Thialfi and his sometimes-named (and as often unnamed) sister. ...One wishes, for Symmetry's sacred sake, that this sister might perhaps have a role to play in the ensuing adventure; and perhaps she will...in these pages, perhaps, and definitely in the inevitable hologram-film of two generations hence; but Schnorri remains silent about her and I believe I shall as well, for now. ...Oh well, the Schnorrer calls her Roskva and at least one Net-snared translator speaks of her "milk-white bosom", cranking up her age?

* * *

Alors, an endless day was passed, trudging along barren tundra, a frozen desert with an eerie absence of landmarks. Eerie because our travelers, the Gods as well as the kids, began to develop a true problem determining any form of perspective...temporal as well as visual. Nothing happened. And the sun seemed fixed in the sky. No mountains towered over them, no lichen decorated the ice-patched ground. For a while, Thor and Loki took to carrying the two human children on their stout shoulders, one on each pair (legs adangle in front), so to move more quickly (the holy goats were swifter than either God); but as they seemed to be making no measurable progress at all, the Gods gave it up, eventually, and set the kids on their own feet again, the party as a whole taking on an humbly human pace. (Although it should be noted that Loki---who now and then seems to betray an awareness of the narrative itself, doesn't he?---, having observed Thialfi's striding out in front of the others, said to Thor, "He moves well, doesn't he?, for a human?" "For a human," Thor echoed, stolidly.)

Then, all of a sudden, with no transition at all, darkness fell.

"These are not 'days' or 'nights' as we know them," said Thor.

"It's self-evident, Thorny," Loki rejoined and lit the torch he'd providently (or knowingly?) brought along.

(9)

Thialfi saw it first: a darker darkness...and tangible, he'd soon find, even soft to his touch. He called back to the others; they approached, torch-led by Loki.

Whatever it was, it was massive, all agreed.

"It blocks our path," Thor pointed out.

"Perhaps it's the 'end in itself' I've read so much about!" Loki mused.

Unlettered in brain-tease, Thor misunderstood this comment as an allusion to one of Loki's monstrous offspring, an outsized serpent, colossal in length and a scourge of humankind, whom Thor himself had quelled by wrapping the critter around the human world, then jamming its hindquarters into its mouth.

That was yawns ago, of course, but it still ranked as one of Thunder's signature gestes. Yep; done Thor a power o' good to reflect on this! It was known, too, that the so-called Midgard Serpent possessed the ability to disguise hisself at will, a gene he inherited from his half-Divine dad. Perhaps this...hugeness was simply a manifestation of the literally self-involved monster, hence of Thor's own reflected glory in having, Time out of mind, subdued it!

"Sorry, Sub-dude," said the Trickster, picking up on Thor's thinking (or, perhaps, reading it here?). "Thanks to you, my little pride 'n' joy circles the *human* domain---offering it form through self-reference, by the way, but don't let that o'er-burden yer brain none. Any case, the point is: we're no longer in Midgard, Dunder. Left it behind, back where Time made sense. Nope, we be now, somewhere!, in Jotenheim! And this soft darkness may prove our first encounter with one of the locals. If it is not, as I say, an 'end in itself'."

Thialfi, for whom all this---even the obscure God-chat---was mystery and high adventure, lit out to the left, disappearing. In no time he returned. "There's an end, all right," the lad reported. (Loki smiled upon the simple human.) "It's round the bend, just out of eyeshot. And beyond that, an opening!"

The four made haste. Darkness had brought an even more stringent chill and with it a biting wind. Gratefully, they entered the vaguely circular opening...and found themselves in a huge atrium of sorts, the walls and floor of which seemed woven, cloth-like; perhaps the ceiling was as well, as Loki's torch-light played over a surface made seemingly of a common substance. Curious!

Almost at once, however, there was a more immediate matter for consideration: wind from the open entry-way flicked a solo spark from the Trickster's torch; up into the air it flitted, landing at the Thunderer's well-shod feet, instantly setting the floor afire. Vigorous stomping from the God's immortal boots put paid to the initial blaze but also succeeded in shaking loose additional sparks from Loki's torch, starting five little fires.

"All right: stop everything!!" Loki commanded.

Shocked, Thor stopped stomping.

"First, I'd douse the source, People, lest we all perish here...by fire, as in the German version." So saying, the Tricky One pulled a canteen from his backpack and poured its contents---mere water, we assume---over the torch. "Now we do the like to the progeny of your brainlessness, Brother God."

And, soon enough, with no further anxiety, all the resultant flamelets were extinguished...and our four characters found themselves in a gelid darkness beyond telling.

"What's next, Dude?" Thor asked, peremptorily. "You seem to be calling the play here."

"We walk, Indian-file, away from the opening, out of the wind, bearing ever-left," Loki answered. "Thor, you lead."

This cheered Thursday's eponym, as he was born to lead and knew it. (His *amour propre* had suffered a bit in the stomping episode, but, as with many a Deity, his emotional memory---in the service, ever, of his ego---was quite short.)

* * *

Then, strangely to summarize, a more-or-less exact sequence took place, five times in a row! Calling for a left turn (as if it were his own idea), Thor led the trio into an ever-narrowing chamber that dead-ended in a wall made of the by-now familiar woven matter. This necessitated clumsily re-assembling the file such that, in proper order with Thor up front, it would retrace its steps, retake the atrium, and move along the atrial wall until another left turn presented itself. Yes, this happened five times, each time more tediously. At the second turning, Thor had said, "Perhaps this will lead to a different outcome," and the others had muttered assent. Thereafter, grim silence reigned.

At length, when all were in the fifth chamber---which resembled the others, save that it was somewhat larger---, Thor declared himself properly bushed. "I can go no further," he stated. "I'm going to doss down in this room: its size suits me. As for the rest of you: we've determined that all these rooms are similarly empty and harmless and out-of-the-wind; cozy, in fact. I suggest that each occupy one of his or her choosing. Tomorrow, when we are all awake, we'll reconnoitre." The kids yawned a silent assent.

"We can leave the fifth chamber unpeopled and call that a sacrifice to the Norns," Loki suggested brightly: "Praise Necessity for what's unneeded!" ...But no one seemed to hear him. Indeed, it was almost beyond the two mortals to crawl into their respective chambers. The goats settled in on either side of their master, who had already begun stertorously to snore. Even Loki had had enough of waking consciousness.

Yes, sleep took hold of all and so overmastering was it that none of the four was more than momentarily disturbed by the periodic rumblings that seemed to shake the very ground on which their internal pentagon rested.

Dreams? Thor's were of an idealized past; in that, the God was no better than nor different from others of his political persuasion (the might-making-right mob), regardless of species. Thialfi's dreams embraced the unknown as a lover. Roskva's I ought not to imagine, as I have denied her any more than a place-holder's place (to date) in this welter-logged saga. And when Loki sleeps, he *never* dreams: he just goes...somewhere else.

(10)

There came a time---as there must in all such tales---when intrusion from an outside world shattered narrative complacency. The last to wake was Thor; himself was the most deeply attached to his dreams (in an emotional sense, that is; a young braveheart like our Thialfi doesn't *need* the delirious hope that saturates his sleep: he is soon to act out his dreams; but the likes of Thor requires the oneiric image of a Golden-Age-lost in order to stay in-character when awake). In reality, the intrusion had been with them all along: the aforementioned rumbling. It had just finally *got through* to them, that's all, gaining the eventual upper hand even with the sleep-besotted Thunderer.

As they, one-by-one, returned to the atrium, the four found it bathed in sunlight.

"It must be tomorrow," Thor announced; once more, Loki rolled his eyes.

"May I again be our scout, Sir?" Thialfi asked, looking up at Thor.

The God was charmed by this deferential address but shook his great, hairy head from side to side. "No, Young Man, I'll be first out. If all is well, I'll make a sign and the rest of you may follow."

* * *

But Thor made no sign: once out, he'd been immediately immobilized and stricken dumb into the bargain. This came not through any apparent enchantment---and certainly not from failure of nerve!---; no, simply put, Thor had witnessed something that rendered him witless.

What the God had beheld and beheard was an improbably gigantic, yet clearly humanoid, figure. It---or he---lay dorsally (facing Thor) on a canvas large enough to outfit an Icelandic armada, his/its huge head cradled in the crook of an elbow, eyes blinkered: the entity was evidently sleeping...which ought to have been more obvious than evident save for the fact that the sounds that escaped the creature's blubbery lips seemed less like snoring than some madcap anticipation of a sonic boom. [I stress its/his seeming species because we humans make all things---Gods 'n' monsters---resemble ourselves; and then claim that they created us! See below.] Yes, next to *these* snores,

Thor's had been those of a dozing kitten---not that he had ever heard himself snoring, of course.

* * *

Having had no word from Thor in some time, Loki shrugged and led the kids out of the atrium. The three came to stand beside their transfixed leader and saw what he saw.

"Well, well," mused Loki as he regarded the literally horizontal figure sprawled out before them. And I mean "literally" quite literally: he/it appeared to extend from horizon to horizon, with the only other local construct an impossibly tall tree, its upper branches sky-high; and, oh yes, a distant mountain.

"And yet," Loki continued [as if he and I were thinking in parallel], "let me try the physical equivalent of a thought-experiment. To our Occidental eyes, the Giant appears impossibly large, I grant. But I suspect that as we narrow the distance between him and us, his size will tend to shrink a bit."

Thialfi took heart at these words. "You mean, "he said: "here in Jotunheim, things only have an absolute size?"

LOKI (instituting Drama): I'm glad **someone** is paying attention! Yes, Boy, hereabouts we seem to lack all perspective. ...If Giant *Kultur* has any art to speak of, I doubt it's enjoyed a Renaissance.

THIALFI: Is it true of Time, too? Yesterday did seem incredibly long! And nothing really happened until the end.

LOKI: Right again, Kid. I tumbled to it last night but I'll spell it out now: we left relativity behind when we exited Midgard. I'm guessing these Giants measure Time---and Space!

---in terms of the events that take place. It might yet be Odin's Day, for all we know. Of course, back in Asgard, where Thor and I hail from, everything's Eternal---

THIALFI (agog): ---"Eternal"!?!

LOKI (mockingly matter-of-fact): *If* only for the moment, yes. So that also differs---if in a different way---from your human reality. But *this*...: this is new to me, too! Interesting.... Yes, let's approach the behemoth and see if we don't ourselves gain stature.

Thor understood none of this colloquy but he knew a call to action when he heard one. With an unnecessary (and unnecessarily silenced) wave of his great arm, Thursday's child led his foursome forward.

(11)

And the Trickster's hunch proved right. Even as the four strode toward the massive figure, they found their strides lengthening, their reach extending. Thialfi looked down...and witnessed the ground retreating beneath his gaze. He looked up and regarded the noisy slumberer. The latter was still very large, yes, but he no longer occupied one's entire visual frame. Even the mountain seemed now a mere hillock and the tree had retreated from its heavenly reaches. Then curiosity made the lad turn turtle and he was instantly rewarded with an accurate estimation of last night's bivouac: it had seemed so much larger in the dark...and then its true form and sometime function dawned on him: "Why...it's a glove!"

Thor followed Thialfi's gaze; the kid was right and it kindled a right resentment in the Deity's breast. Seeing that Giant cut down to size but with a size that yet promised menace, and, realizing that he'd still be lost in dreams were it not for this creature's infernal snoring, Thor fell back on his basic answer to *everything*: he jerked out his hammer.

The next sequence would be most harmlessly portrayed by an animated cartoon of the early, innocent variety where any amount of raw physical violence can take place to no great effect. Thor took aim dead-center the Giant's massive brow and let fly; he watched with satisfaction as the hammer disappeared into its target before returning to his hand. The God glowed with self-love.

But what happened next was untoward. His huge adversary gently bestirred himself, shook his great head in mild irritation, and asked, "Has one of the leaves from yon tall tree floated down upon my forehead?" He glanced up, then continued, "No, 'tis not in leaf. Ah, well, a mystery; back to sleep then!"

Thor was aroused to anger. "**He** gets to sleep," the God bellowed, "and meantime---thanks to him!---I'm stuck in Reality!!", thus establishing, for all Time?, the priority of this Deity's desires. "We'll see how lightly he takes *this* blow!"

So saying, Thunder reared back and launched his missile with the force of a full-fledged tornado. ...But this effort failed even to wake the Giant; oh, several snores came out more like snorts, but then respiration resolved into a maddeningly regular, clearly peaceful cadence, once again.

Now Thor found himself exasperated, stymied as seldom before in life. *Never* had his beloved Mjollnir (for he had nicknamed his tool as a human male will his penis) proved so ineffectual. But fortunately for the triune nature of fairy tales, the God's mental make-up was devoid of imagination, so he couldn't think of how to deal with this novel situation beyond trying the same thing, once again!

Once again! This time---winding up, as in an Olympian hammer-throw of more recent vintage---, Thor put all his strength, all his self-belief, yea, the totality of his being into the hurl, such that he actually felt *himself* entering the Giant's cranium, fancied himself buried in the Giant's brain. (This were no unexpectedly-imaginative feat: to Thor it felt *real.*) So deeply had he plunged into the identity of another that it took several moments for little Mjolnir to be reunited with its master...and several more for Thor to realize that the death he thought he'd dealt was itself nonexistent: for the Giant stood before him, arms akimbo.

(12)

"So...is that how you Aesir wake each other up?" the Giant queried his company, a fine mockery playing about his lips: "By a tentative tapping upon the forehead? Yes, I recognize you: you're 'Gods'. And I see you have brought some human slaves with you. Or do you consider them your pets? Tut-tut. We Giants don't hold with that practice, by the way; yeah, you've got some evolving to do! Yes, you are larger than your humans. But to a Giant, you see, 'size' is exquisitely relative. And whatever's relative really can't be discussed in absolute terms. And *those* terms are all we really care about."

LOKI: Hmm.... Nicholas of Cusa?

THE GIANT: In fact, I reckon you don't know that my kind don't even call ourselves "Giants". We're just really big men, that's all. But we've learned to treat all life-forms with a rough equality: and that distinguishes us. A man's a man, for all that...and all that.

THIALFI (boldly): Dude doesn't half run his mouth, does he? [To the Giant:] Listen, Mister, you're in the presence of Thor-of-Asgard! You might want to watch your words.

THOR (to Thialfi): Hush, Lad. Mind your betters.

* * *

...Alas, my Reader, it was true!! In common with more common bullies, Alpha dominance masked a canine, Trumpish respect for authority. What his hammer couldn't obliterate, Thor worshipped. Thialfi was thrown for the loop-of-loops; he hung his head.

[In fact, some bardic scholars date the birth of Humanism to Thialfi's disappointment in Thor.]

"So...," mused the Giant, all condescension, "this rag-tag party, so effin' far from home: where is it bound?"

Quoth Thor, tugging an imaginary forelock, "An it please you, Your Grace, we may already have arrived. For Jotunheim was our only goal and it's apparently apparent [Quailing at the Giant's size and seeming strength]...that we are **there**. [Groveling yet more abjectly; gulping] How...how does one address thee?"

"Oh, you may call me Skrymir, for the nonce," said the Giant, "nonsense though that be," seeking to turn a phrase? "But kindly do not judge my kind by me; I am the least of those my brethren. As it is Jotunheim you would experience, you must needs encounter it in its concentrated form: our capital city, yclept Utgard. There you will experience Gianthood in florid overplus: Gigantic logic, Gigantic *Kultur.* ...Again, I use your word for us strictly as a basis for comparison: for comparison---I'm well aware---is the best your minds can conjure. [Mock-reflectively:] Have I developed colonitis?

LOKI (somehow uncowed): "Screamer", is it?

SKRYMIR: That's right, pseudo-phonetically.

LOKI: Hm. Unless you're lying about that, it does scotch a little theory I'd developed about you.

SKRYMIR: When one is a huge presence in a world of pygmies 'n' punies, he finds little need to lie, none to exaggerate! [Yawns luxuriantly; all are drawn by his inspiration, then buffeted by the out-breath] Now, where's my left-hand glove? I seem to have mislaid it. ...But let us hear your wrong-headed theory, Handsome. I'm all ears.

LOKI: 'Tis simple. You'd turn out the author of this tale--- its collator, anyway---, one Schnorri Sturluson. The tip-off being the monstrous sounds you make when unconscious. ...You'd not be the first author to include himself as a character. And Jesus founded his church upon a pun, as Joyce pointed out.

SKRYMIR: I, the author?! Ho-ho!! Only if he or she identify with me! And now I know who YOU are, by the way. [Looks about himself] Where's that missing glove?

LOKI: Perhaps it's happy, as the Zemblans aver.

SKRYMIR: Read 'im already. Sorry, Trickster: thou beholdest in me a past master of the treacherous narrative. Can't top Grampa!; don't try. [Sternly] You'll never be loved,

Loki, because you're *no one thing*. Have you not noticed?: identity forms the basis of all relations worth the name: the proof by identity!: relations relate. This were sometime a tautology...but it gets blindly approved, rubber-stamped, time after time. Leaving the likes of you a land-locked country, forever inhospitable to visitors. No, nobody can get a handle on you. Oh, you'll prove a hit in post-Modernity, you wait around that long. But that's a pretty skimpy day-in-the-sun, Bro. Yeah, as eras go, you'll find that post-Modern Times---that briefest of briefs wherein *commentary* rules?: t' will be over before you know it! And even then, you'll only be *acknowledged*; you'll never generate any warmth, any fervor. You'll simply be recognized: an avatar of irresponsibility in an era that **strives** for that state. Yes, I know YOU!

LOKI: I---

SKRYMIR: You think your thoughts original; but all you do is quote others'. [Sissy voice:] And *comment....* [Stern again:] Meantime, at the moment, all your flash has accomplished is a bog in the story-line.

LOKI: I---

SKRYMIR: And the nerve of you!: trying to make Forrester feel guilty about the very sin you typify! You may not care about keeping your Reader but, I assure you, your Narrator does!

LOKI: I---

SKRYMIR: Here's the locus of the problem: the Giant-in-you embraces death-as-truth. You make it part of your patter. But your true Giant?: he *lives it!*

LOKI: I---

THOR: Excuse me, Mister Screamer, Sir, but I can tell you where your glove is.

SKRYMIR: As the wheels turn at last! Yes, where is it, Little Big Guy?

THOR: It's a few versts behind the four of us, Sir. We...we slept in its fingers, last night. Quite comfortably too, thank you. I mean: *thank* you!

SKRYMIR: Don't mention it. [Peers over the four, then reaches over them---casting a vast shadow (our four shiver)---and picks up the glove, dons it] Now...let's be off. We've another literal journey before I go my way and you, yours. I'll meet you at a crossroads, the first you'll encounter; wait for you there. It's hard by the outskirts of Utgard. And in case hunger gnaws, *en route*, feel free to dip into my wallet---it's replete with Utgardian delicacies.

* * *

With that, *soi-disant* Skrymir delved deep into the rear pocket of his robe and produced a roan-leather oblong, cinched with mauve ribbons, which he flipped carelessly over to Thor. The God staggered under its weight, dropping to one knee, but kept the "wallet" from falling to earth.

"Thankee mightily, Sir," said he. And then, to his troops in an altogether-predictably-brutal tone: "You heard Mister Screamer! We break camp and prepare to move out. Now!"

...But my Reader ought not to fall into Thialfi's error. His hero had *not* lost heart...and, hence, the key to his character. Nay; momentarily he'd lost far more than that: what Thor had lost was *the place*.

(13)

Oh, it were a sad parade that made its way across the unforgiving plains of Jotunheim, that day. Thor would start to feel good about himself after, say, issuing an unnecessary command or two; then he'd spot the Giant, 'way off in the sameness of an undoubted, flat future, and was reminded how thoroughly he'd been put in his place. Even after Skrymir had so outpaced our quartet as to be beyond their horizon, Thor would note some seemingly purposeful reminder---a squashed bush, a footprint all four could fit inside---and feel again his selfish version of the agenbite of inwit: what passes for conscience in a God.

As for Thialfi, with his pole-star in eclipse, he'd thoroughly *lost it*. He who had ever been a forerunner could scarcely summon a trudge.

Loki, for the first time in his born days, found himself tongue-tied, nay, mind-tied, strangely denied access not only to his forever-jaded sense of the inevitable, but, yea, even to **me!**, his sometime maker. Non-creative by nature (and predilection?), he had hitherto always had the ability to scramble onto the plane of reference, there to witness reality as I would pretend it to be. Once I set it down, it was his, enjoying less a "life" than a *commentary.* [You were hip to that.] No more. Skrymir, somehow, had severed the connection. And so Loki--- again, in a moment without parallel---found himself *going through the motions.*

And Roskva, ignored even now, kept her own counsel.

Let us leave them to it.

* * *

Oh, wait, there was one event of note during this seemingly (being-ly!) endless day. [Is it *still* Wednesday?, JF asks himself.] When all agreed that they were feeling hunger more deeply than, for example, frustration, disappointment, futility, unfairness, trepidation, impatience, shame, or boredom, Thor ordered a lunch break and set about attempting to untie the ribbons that bound the Giant's weighty gift---which, by the way, the quondam Thunderer had borne on his tired shoulders ever since setting out, that day. But the ribbons wouldn't give, wouldn't!, wouldn't!! Nor could they be axed into pieces, for he tried that next, borrowing Loki's blade...but it wouldn't serve.

At length, hefting his inviolate load once again, Thor commanded, "Break's over! Let's take to the road again! We'll ask the Boss to unwrap his Xmas present, once we hit the crossroads."

Reader: did you note some hope, here? You were meant to. For he of the lumbering thought-processes was, oh-so-languidly, synthesizing his hunger with his sense of failure: a conversion to purpose that neither could have achieved on its own. And purpose is the source of all energy, even in the Godhead. Let's be present: Thor's sense of self has taken a thrashing, yes; but his courage remains undiminished---a good thing: he'll need it. I mean: you'll need him to need it.

Does this seem nought but a rationalization? Remember, Reader, we are speaking not of men but of Gods.

(14)

What it saw?

This time, our weary famished quartet suspected what it saw, although taking an opposed form, to be some species of optical illusion. Suspected and, collectively, sighed---both from tedium at its predictable trickery and in relief at its presage. For, this time, in spotting the Giant, they saw him seem merely as large as he had been when last among them, even though a tedious distance separated seers from seen. Hence, no one was made perceptually uncomfortable by the fact that the size of self-named Skrymir varied not at all as they approached him, stomachs grumbling as one. [Schnorri's story, by this point, has left behind Thor's ever-replenishing goats---sudden cousins to Al Capp's Schmoos!---and I shan't deviate from the text.] No, what did disturb the four, diminish them in all but number, was the Giant's immediate display of lavish pity:

"Welcome, all! I see you were unable to open my wallet," were Skrymir's first words, his huge face working in attitudes of concern too exaggerated to be dismissed out of hand. "That's on me. It slipped my massive mind that my wallet's binding might be beyond thy picking. Drefful sorry! What can I say in self-exculpation? With great memory comes great forgetfulness?"

None of our four answered. All panted, almost silently.

"Hmm. Well. Let's eat!" said Skrymir and, with a nimble flourish, flicked off the ribbons of his mighty wallet and laid a bloomin' banquet before the four. "Dig in, Chicklets," said he.

"I've picnicked already. Time on my hands, waitin' fer our round-view. Oh, I know: y'all were movin' as speedily as your clipped appendages could manage. Any road, this here spread is all your'n. When yer sated, I'd advise a restorative snooze under yon spreadin' elm. An' when ye get movin' again, take this here right fork. It'll lead ye to Utgard's Servants' Entrance. 'N' don't get yer knickers in a twist about that! If'n ye entered by way of the Great Gate, immediate greatness would be demanded of thee. 'N' from what I gather, you'd be...safer if ye present yerselves as willing to *serve*, rather'n aimin' to impress, mmm?"

"Thonkoo! Thonkoo, Scweamuh!" quoth Thor, mouth crammed with food.

"I'll be off then," said Skrymir and headed left, tossing these words over his shoulder: "Oh and one more thing?: your impressions---and your Fabulist's quandary---nonwithstanding, **it is still Wednesday!**"

"Whot a guy!!" said Thor, between chomps.

This was answered with silence; and, in time, with various noises betokening surrender to contented slumber.

(15)

Yet all woke up in profound discontent; and hungry with it! Yes, it was as if the Giant's spread---so generously laid on, so greedily gobbled---had proved naught but virtual, containing but nugatory nourishment. As if, in consuming it, our quartet had merely been reacting to flavor, smell, and taste, not to mention the sumptuous visuals. Not that any had noticed, at the time. Ah, but now, Gods and humans alike awoke feeling as though they had not eaten at all, not for days.

Loki, whose appetites ran deepest ('I am all urge,' his one honest reflection), considered grimly that his entire consciousness had come to center on a single, gut-twisting pang. Yet he seemed the least surprised of the four and this had its compensations: 'A predictably-nasty prediction of 21st Century foodism,' he mused; and this precognition lit his comely features: he knew where his Narrator was coming from. As for Thor, he'd yet to meet a deprivation he couldn't reconstrue as Divine nutrition for his lordly ego. And so, between the two of 'em, the Gods were able to conjure just enough ergs to get their party on the road once more.

As to the humans: for a second time (and after sharing a shrug) the Gods heaved 'em onto their relatively broad shoulders and more or less *wore* them there, as scanty fur-pieces. (Only "relatively"? Thor, while trudging, found it difficult entirely to dismiss how thoroughly Skrymir had belittled him. Yet Loki ---and even Thialfi---had somewhy endowed the Giant homeland with the power to obliterate perspective, if he'd heard their palaver aright. So, perhaps, Thor's belittlement was all in his own head?, and, hence, inappropriate?; or so our ponderous Lumberer mused.)

* * *

Utgard, as the two-plus-two approached it, presented as a walled city ('*Ein feste Burg,*' thought Lutheran Loki) and was familiarly immense; that is: impossibly immense, then truly immense, and, eventually, merely immense. This declension comforted Thor. Following orders, he and they disregarded the infinitely imposing Great Gate and soldiered on until their arc-ing path brought 'em to the one marked SERVANTS. "*Non serviam,*" muttered Luciferian Loki, but was his heart in it?

Thor, becoming quite accustomed by now to attempting physical feats that lay beyond his sinew, was less than shocked at his inability to prise apart the bars that discouraged *entrée* (even for servants?) into this truly "gated" community. Nor could he more than jiggle the thick metal rod that lay athwart the inner surface of these bars.

His half-brother's failure, however, was always meat-'n'-drink to Loki and, instantly shedding that dimension unnecessary to a fictional character, the newly Two-D Trickster wormed easily between the bars and, his depth restored, handily undid the crosspiece that had been Thor's jiggling frustration. (Restored, as well, was Loki's sexy sense-of-self.)

Thus did the four enter Utgard, not even as servants but, to all appearances, as thieves.

(16)

And, to all *immediate* appearances, the city they entered comprised but one---truly Gigantic---building. Their eyes couldn't take it all in. (Loki reasoned: 'Perhaps the main gate gives onto a courtyard; but servants pass directly from outside to inside?')

They heard, indistinctly, the far-off sound of a jangled choral-singing and cautiously moved toward it.

* * *

Our heroes remained un-greeted as they made their way through larger and yet larger rooms, finally fetching up in a cathedral of a space (that is: its immensity emphasized by its boundaries). Here was gathered a chorus of perhaps a thousand

Giants, each one seemingly larger than his fellow (an odd form of visual reciprocity when concentrated upon), that our wised-up weary ones recognized intermediately as yet another illusion. Suspended above was a sort of dais, on which reposed (enthroned) the largest Giant of all, a creature whose head was held so far aloft as to be and to remain invisible both to the Deified and to the human perspectives, despite necks craned to the creaking point.

When this man/monster sang, however, the sound approached not as a blast from on high but with an insidious intimacy, a tonal whisper, as if these Giants were already hip to that late-20th Century audio technology capable of "grading" an arena's volume from the v.i.p. boxes to the bleacher-creature tiers.

The song sung was certainly odd enough, although it hewed closely to an eventually-traditional form: the leader (as implied, a past-master of under-playing) croaked its verses while the Giant masses belted out the chorus. Three examples of the former will be given here and one, naturally, of the latter.

[The words will be Angled but one's Reader should imagine a clotted cackling, rising and falling in volume, stuffed to the gills with rough consonants. The pitches are completely random, hence only coincidentally harmonic: this was not music. Perhaps, when the story sees print, I can align the tub-thumping rhythmic stresses...in a hieratic erratum slip? Meantime: count four beats a line.]

LEADER (crack/crooned in Ur-Gigantic):

"Meaning"? [1 beat / ½ beat] There is no

meaning. [1 beat / ½ beat] For we have

found that we are bound to lose the

place, what e'er we do. [1]

"Freedom"? [1 beat / ½ beat] There is no

freedom. [1 beat / ½] For who would

choose to sing the blues, if by that

act---that tactless act!---she'd be de-

nied a state of Grace?

CHORUS (shout/sung in Ur-G): Oh we a-

gree! [2 beats] We a-

gree! [1 beat / ½] There simply

is [1/2]no simpler way to

be. [2] We *af-*

firm the present [1/2 beat]and

wish it well: [1/2] a

sweet damnation; [1/2] our

bless-ed, curs'd creation, [1/2] our

Heavenly Hell. [1/2] Hoo-

ray!!! [3]

LEADER:

"Heartless"?[1 beat / ½] You think us

Heartless? [1 beat / ½] We merely

recognize [1] that our

lives are going to end! [1]

"Myst'ry"? [1 beat / ½] There is no

myst'ry. [2] For the

hist'ry of the world's enough to

send us 'round the bend. [1/2] "Com-

passion"? [1 beat / ½] There's no com-

passion. [1 beat / ½] You worship

Fashion ev'ry time you bow your

head. [3]

"Living"? [1 beat / ½] You think you're

living?[1 beat / ½] Why, next to

me you'll quickly see [1/2]: you

shoulda stayed in bed!

CHORUS: Oh we agree [etc.]

LEADER:

Nowhere![1 beat / ½] You're heading

nowhere!! [1 beat / ½]   And so are

we but you see we're *a-*

ware that that's our goal. [1 beat]

"Answers"? [1beat / ½] There are no

answers. [2 beats] Only

questions and suggestions and a

ton of rig'marole!

CHORUS: Oh we agree, etc. [Ends with:] Hoo-

ray! [1/2] Hooray! [1/2] Hoo-

ray for TODAY!!! [1]

(17)

That was, again, a translation. The original was sung in an arcane tongue which, of our four cast-aways, Loki alone could rightly ken. The others were all at sea, hearing only a Dramatic babble. Hence, when the singing ceased, it was he, Loki, who stepped forward and addressed the head-hidden leader...and in the critter's own lingo.

LOKI (in Ur-Gigantic): It's clear enough that your lyricist respects only the absence of perspective. And that you yourself embody that sought-after point of view. And that you have somehow laid your local Reality upon the procrustean bed of your desire. It strikes a chord within me.

H-H LEADER (in Ur-G): **And**...equally clear that you, Fellow, are none other than that consummate counter-identity freak, that celestial con-person, that cypher in both senses, Loki of Asgard, he who never took a side he didn't intend ultimately to betray. Greetings---both profound and somehow superficial---, Mister Fish-nor-fowl!

LOKI (in Ur-G): And you would be...?

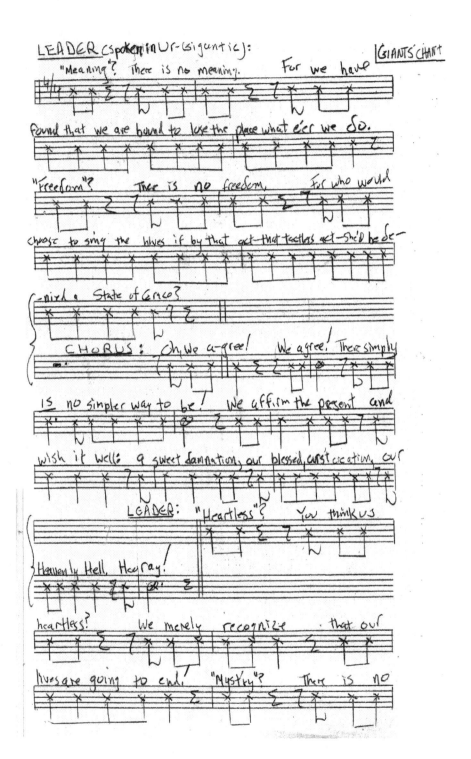

H-H LEADER (in Ur-G): Well-phrased, Trickster! Here in Utgard, all are as they would be. And you share that strand with us, that genial if twisted tendency, unwilling as you may be to embrace your inner Giant. But I...? I am the self-appointed point, as it were: the reason you are here. Oh, I'm quite aware of precisely why you have graced us with this visit, be in no doubt about that. ...But let us not conduct this colloquy, you and I, in terms exclusive to ourselves. Your colleagues---check 'em out!---stand around, stupefied, "kickin' the sand out there", as Lord Buckley put it. ...And besides, we only share a common tongue because of your Narrator's misreading of Chomsky: deep glamor? Let's get intelligible, don't you think?? Your Thor's beginning to look bored---treacherous for a God. Switch to good Reader's English, shall we?

LOKI (in Ur-G): Insh'Allah.

* * *

And with that Loki turned to the Thunderer and shrugged, somewhat shame-facedly.

Thor looked his handsome half-brother in the eye and demanded, "What's up? Right there at the end I heard my name mentioned."

Loki shrugged again and gestured feebly at their headless host, as if to say: 'His game. His rules.'

"That's right!" said the über-Giant, interpreting (correctly) the gesture. And if, broadcasting in Ur-G, his words had seemed poured into the porches, when Englished his voice took on an eerie echo, at once both boomed and whispered, by turns indifferent and intimate.

"Word travels fast," he continued. "...You'll have to pardon that trite locution. And many another, I fear: behind my back, my fellow Jints refer to me as the King of Cliché: a shout-out to Pee Wee?" (He chortled, setting up a downright deafening sympathetic-titter among his multitude; our four held their ears until it stopped.) "To cases, then: I am Utgard-Loki. And, yes, I know who you are, word traveling fast. Or, at least, I can identify your sharpest mind---which I've already encountered--- and, before that and yet 'way beyond it, your strongest and most self-evident appearance. ...We are cartoonists, we Giants: we pick out the most obvious presentation and let it do agency for the whole. Caricature: it helps us obliterate perspective, ever our goal...: what you were on about earlier, Li'l Loki. ...Anybody in the audience from Schenectady?"

LOKI (in English): Cynic-douche?

UTGARD-LOKI: A touch broad but not too bad. No, but what I meant was: you're not even in the picture, Trackstar, the field of vision. To us, to a true Giant, you dissolve into the far grander Being at your side. Pronounced characteristics are all we take in. ...And, in service to this, our concept of perception as a process of extrapolation from grotesque exaggeration, I mindfully welcome YOU, Thor, to Jotunheim!, you of the legendary sinew and mental density.

(18)

But something in this odd binaural address stung our principal hero into unthinking bravery...which was, of course, his default setting. Here was a wrong to be righted, even if the conflict was merely verbal. ('And it were weak,' he subjuncted, 'to fear aught that I can't even see in its entirety. Lose face before a faceless being?')

"Your welcome is difficult to swallow," he began. "You address us as one being. We are not. We...are distinct individuals."

U-L: Quite.

"I say we are," retorted the Thunderer.

U-L: Tut-tut. You may justly expect to be ignored throughout Jotunheim, Thor, if you continue to disdain our chosen form of dialogue.

"Yes, well, for our part, we cannot be Dramatic **all the time**," Thor countered, knowing himself opposed, if utterly unsure of his ground, or even of what he was saying. "Our deeds stand in no need of heightening."

U-L (amused): You'd not fall back on indirect discourse? My tongue may be Greek to you but, believe me, yours is Barbaric to us!

Thor thought about that: "Indirect discourse"; what could that mean? "No," he allowed aloud, "that's beyond me." Then he said the next thing to pop into his head: "But simple quotation will do."

Loki stared in disbelief at his brother-once-repelled: 'Am I witnessing the birth of intuition?', keeping that thought to himself.

U-L (with a minatory chuckle): Questions of courtesy aside, you might consider, Thor, whether you are in any position to impose your forms on our speech. You are far from home.

LOKI (doubly-impressed despite himself): The dude has a point, Dunder. Is this really where you'd take a stand? And on the merest quibble?

THOR (irascibly, as if he knew what he were about): Oh, all right. I'll mount the stage.

U-L (immediately): Smart move! Now then: you say you are individuals. So, distinguish yourselves! No one gets to hang in Jotenheim, save he---or she or it---can display some marked talent or genius. Thor is known to us. Loki too...although we consider him all mouth, the soul of negligibility, cutting capers in the greater God's shadow.

THOR: I---

U-L: Take praise where you find it, please. ...But perhaps I am selling you short, all of you, singular or plural. Yes, perhaps you even have it within you to throw down a challenge to our Gigantic style of perception, of perception as theory-of-knowledge.

LOKI (directly to the Reader): 'E pissed 'em all off!

U-L (to Loki): Mere addle-essence, Handsome. Yer Reader ain't in it for the surd-play. [To Thor:] So, tell me, Most Ruthless of Gods, what can these others do, that they may justify their being here, hmmm??? "Individuals"? How am I wrong in regarding the four of you as little more than an unholy amalgam of myth-raddled humanity and two of its toothy, too-typical projections? ...But a Giant is generous, large: I never mind being *proven* wrong. I'm all ears: what *can* they do...to win a Giant's attention?

(19)

Silence held; and Drama gave way, if briefly, to its unimaginable opposite. Then, like a missed cue, Loki's stomach began---ominously, extravagantly, noisily!---to rumble. This "answer" to Utgard-Loki's challenge struck the Giant masses as stupendously funny and they launched into yet another deaf-making roar, our heroes once again holding their ears. But the roaring ceased the moment their leader extended a policeman's palm.

U-L (as Drama resumes): Shall I do your thinking for you? Yes, we Giants perceive our selves as we do the world. In so doing, we assume an integrity 'way beyond your ability to idealize the quality. We would *not* be "individuals". Every manjack of us represents some aspect of our common being. We are *all* Utgard-Loki. Ask anyone here and he'll affirm it. I am merely the summary of those aspects. ...But, laughter aside, I find I am obliged to treat your answer with due gravity, *mon petit* Locus or Locust. Are you somehow advanced in your swallowing capacity?; can you eat up a storm?; is that your true talent: spectacular gluttony?

LOKI: I am hungry.

U-L: I *love* ego-as-deference! [To his minions:] No, don't start laughing again. ...And, one-of-you: skip down to the Oxydation State-room and haul up *Logi*. He's the one we want for this. Yes!; we'll have a contest of consonants. Others: set up two parallel trestles, yea-long, and heap up both with as much edible grub as may be crammed therein. Hop to it!

(20)

And, soon enough, so it was. According to Schnorri, the wooden trestles extended to one-eighth of a mile (although perhaps the Giant's penchant for denied exaggeration likewise extended to its historian); as for the piled delicacies, the Reader must substitute whatever her own hunger hungers for, just now. Loki stood athwart one trestle, his opponent---a flame-bearded rubicundity---the other. [In the Classics Illustrated version I read as a child, there was but a single trestle with Loki and Logi starting at opposite ends. Reader may opt as her optics desire.] At a signal, lost to recall, both began to eat.

Our Trickster put his head down, appetite *über Alles*, allowing himself but one mid-meal musing: 'I'll undoubtedly win this contest, going away...but I can only hope these Giants maintain a tidy, nearby vomitorium!'

Utterly concentrated and on-task, Loki was oblivious to the beating waves of shouted encouragement bestowed upon his rival; heard nothing of Thor's outrage, his yellish questioning of the "rules of engagement" and the noisy mirth this evoked. No, Loki kept his attention centered squarely on the food. [And, as John Cage once wrote (in a letter to your author), "Attention-placement determines mind."]

So it came about that the Surpriser---yet another of Loki's many eponyms---got the surprise of his life (to date) when, upon reaching the far end of the trestle and, after having consumed every Friggan morsel of food the structure had held, Consonant K looked up only to find himself face-to-face with his counterpart, G. 'Oh, well,' thought the half-God, 'at least I've established a rough parity between our species.'

Imagine his lordly dismay, then, when further eye-balling revealed that his grinning, full-blooded competitor ('A shit-faced grin,' thought Loki unkindly) had not only himself gobbled up all that was in *his* trestle, but had somehow consumed the trestle itself.

Astonied, Loki found his urge to barf stifled. Rendered nearly autistic to his environment, he only woke up when he became aware of Thor's bellowed indignation. ...Can a congenitally-disloyal half-Giant find himself *touched* when a brother acts brotherly? Oh, momentarily. Loki moved immediately to quell Thor's rage. "Chill, Dander," he said. "The dude's appetite lay beyond mine, that's all. **And** his facility to realize it: his chops, literally! ...And something else, Man: there hasn't been time to tell you---they really stir the plot here in Jotunheim!---but you definitely *showed me something* when you stood up to the Giant-of-Giants. I must admit I didn't know you had the loneliest clue about what allowed this whole number to be struck up; the way-shaping form of it, I mean."

"Oh, I don't," Thor admitted. "It's just that I felt, deeply within me, some true opposition...for the first time? It's long been held that these...people [Gesturing warily about him] are our eventual enemies. I felt something of that eventuality, that future, and it put words in my mouth! I felt...dis-authenticated and that sat ill with me, Loki. **I don't** know what's going on. I just went ahead anyway."

'Hm,' thought Loki. 'That's likely why the script referenced Cage while my head was in the trough. Hope that doesn't presage some cockamamie Salute to the Random, Enthronement of Chance! ...Still, maybe the vague acknowledgment of his unavoidable death---however obscure and interlarded with ego---has made my brave, dim brother into more than he was?'

(21)

UTGARD-LOKI: Garsh, Guys, sorry to break up this touching, bromantic moment.   But are you'ns [Pronounced in 50s Pittsburgh as "yoonz", the vowels sounded as in "goods" or "hood"---JF] ready to compound failure with itself and thereby to **learn**? What else would you-plural "individuals" claim to do? The girl, I see, you have suppressed, after the manner of your kind; she's barely mentioned.   ...Or shall we lay that at the feet of our highly interruptive Narrator? In any case, what about the human boy? What's his skill?

LOKI: He's fast.

U-L: Is he now! Fleet-of-foot, I take you to mean.

LOKI: Yes. We encountered one of your kind earlier on this our Hejiran jaunt. Big strapping fellow, wide stride. The boy Thialfi was the only one of us who could come near keeping up with the dude. And he scouted for us, Thialfi did. We entrusted our spatial future to him. He gets ahead of himself.

U-L: Beyond the curve, is he? Well, we'll test that. We've got a lad here in Jintland who's so fast he hasn't been named yet! ...Although he answers, at times, to *Hugi.*

* * *

Commands were issued and a race-course set up: your standard oval but running around the inner perimeter of the city wall, a wall indistinguishable from the building it enclosed.

[Loki, eager to pick up Class cues, had erred in presuming a courtyard: there was none.] Hence, this race would be an indoor event, albeit an odd one, in that the participants would only be visible when the course led them through the Throne Room. As it would and did. [...It would be difficult, in such a race, **not** to get ahead of oneself.]

UTGARD-LOKI: Enough effin' narration! Let's call it a "carcass" race and let it begin!!

(22)

And so it did.

Thialfi would later comment that he was never actually granted an unobstructed anterior view of his rival. In lieu of an anachronistic starter's gun, a similarly-dubious checkered flag had been waved; but while the two had crouched side-by-side, Thialfi was illuminated by torchlight while the unnamed one (Hugi?) was wrapped in deep shadow. Both immediately disappeared from public view.

Then, scant minutes later, Thialfi emerged from the far side of the Throne Room and chased his own tail up to the starter's table, all smiles, confident of victory. But when he got there, he found the Generic Giant waiting for him: a pulsating silent shadowy outline, a nebulous *Gestalt* but, for all that, an easy winner.

Typical Gigantic ridicule had also greeted Thialfi's arrival. And Utgard-Loki, ever-avid to rub an inferior's nose in it, called immediately for a re-run. The result was a carbon-based copy.

Yet again---this time oozing a spurious mock-Humanist compassion---the Giant's Giant would have the race done over, over. "Give the lad another chance," he said. "He wouldn't have taken this on had he lacked an 'extra gear', somewhere within. You'll see: this time, he will silence our haughty frivolity."

And, oddly to relate, even though losing for a third time, Thialfi heard no laughter as he crossed the finish line. He'd gone all out, indeed had discovered that "extra gear", and a final spurt had actually enabled him to catch sight of his rival's back, just as the latter was crossing over to victory....

Externalizing the viewpoint, it was *this sight*--- the two runners within the same visual frame---that quieted the crowd, muted its mockery, quelled its crowing.

(23)

But Utgard-Loki responded to this somehow-nervous silence with the brutality of a radio talk-show host concerned about dead-air time.

U-L: All right, all right; I can speak for myself! ...Hey, Thoracic/Thurassic! All along, Dino-Dude, we've deemed **you** the one true Being among your lot, here; the others being mere creatures of Time, shadows, animated memory. But we can't class *you* among the Fallen, can we? So we've got some Celestial trials to put you through. But, before we essay the main event, as I view it, I reckon you wouldn't mind wettin' yer whistle? Now, I know you Aesir to be confirmed mead-heads and *that* our larders lack. But we got us some fine Jotunheimer ale that'll uncurl yer short-hairs. What say?

THOR: Bring it on!

U-L: It's more a matter of bringing it *out*, m'Boy. [His huge left hand gesturing toward stage left, where a covered table has been wheeled into view; atop it sits a long, white drinking horn, apparently fashioned of bone, its base swathed in blue table-cloth, and carved up-and-down with all kinds of, yet again!, runic rhyme. Utgard-Loki resumes, ruminantly:] Beating Time, am I? Ah, well: some were not born to be His Master's Voice, eh Victor? [Shakes his huge nether self] To the matter at hand, then! Thor, me Lad, heft that bony corno and cope with its contents! Drink your fill! Your true Giant can drain that horn in one long draught, your pretender in two. The least-hardy of these my fellahin require three. We yearn to know a **God's** capacity!

Thor lifted the carven horn, grasping it at the business end. He couldn't ascertain the horn's overall length as much of it was obscured by its swaddling clothes; but it felt light to the touch: 'Can't be all that much juice in it,' he reflected and put spout to lips.

Immediately, the God's keen taste buds sent self-messages of keener disappointment. 'Tasteless?' he registered. 'Insipid? Adulterated to within an itch of its presumed original substance?' Followed by a more pointed conclusion: 'One expects far more from an arch-enemy. This cannot be their good stuff. Are we held so unworthy?, served watered-down water?' Yet, all the while, drinking while thinking: determined, Thor was, to drink the horn dry, notwithstanding its fluid's shocking insipidity. One kinda kinder thought: 'If this be what Giants drink, so be it!' And one tactical directive: 'Know thy enemy.' And on and on until St. Sanity stepped in: 'Surely, I have drained the sucker! This moisture I feel yet about my mouth must either be illusion ---the phantom limb tendency of habit to form convincing images of its urges---or even some form of reflux, issuing from me myself.'

Arguing thus *to* himself [In verbal form, courtesy of your Narrator, of course], Thor stopped swallowing and closed his mouth.

UTGARD-LOKI: Lift its lid, Boy. See how you did!

Thor did so and was chagrinned to realize that the level of its fluid seemed to have fallen not-at-all. This rudely-nugatory result (and the God's simple astonishment in registering it) evoked predictable chortles, all 'round. And, as with Thialfi's "carcass race", a run-through yielded an identical outcome, right down to the next-to-last laugh.

Our principal hero experienced the emotion of defeat: 'If I cannot even consume at their level, how am I supposed to produce?, how to contend with them in battle? They are Giants, indeed.' And, with that, the Sunderer sank deeply within himself. ...But when you're not all that deep, the surface is never very far away: all it took was an insult to revive our God! Reader: Read on....

UTGARD-LOKI: I've a thought, Thoreau!! Reach under the table and draw forth the device you'll find there.

Meekly, the God did as ordered. Not that he understood what he had in hand, once he'd brought it to light: a weighty object with a pot-belly and a tapered end to which a length of hose was attached, the girth of it girt by a big-assed leather belt.

THOR (momentarily the soul of insecurity): What is it?

U-L: Oh, it may be understood as akin to a hologram: each part containing the whole. Or to what will become known as Black Holes. Or it may be taken as a reified image of this total process that the likes of you and me---not to mention our Nervous Narrator and our?/his? Stalwart Reader---are all caught up in. Yes. But to me, Thor, it's simply a *pisser*, of course: it enables one to continue drinking without distraction. It's for our wee ones, you see: we find it useful in Gigantic toilet training...and to instill a fear of elephantiasis. Strap it on, My Man! ...Of course, you'll have to unbutton, first.

Thor's gorge rose against the idea. He dropped the device with a resounding *clang!* and, in the same gesture, yanked the neck of the drinking horn---as if he would (or could?) strangle it ---and angrily drew it to him. He could hold his piss with the best of 'em and he **knew** it. [Reader: look thereupon for the difference between knowledge and true opinion.]

Well, and then---perhaps for the first time in his mythic life--- the God concentrated his entire being on a task at hand. Yes, there was that committed hammer-toss, wasn't there?; but *this* were a moment wondrous to relate!, for all life about Thor seemed suddenly to cease---and not just for the concentrator himself but for all present [and even for me]. Yes, even narration it-self ground to a halt as, presumably [with the likes of me all at once on the outside, looking in; barred perceptual entry], the chugging continued. [Perhaps the Reader should herself take a bathroom break?]

But all ends must, somewhen, come to an end. This must be stated, even if it rush us unseemly fast to the sole "moral" behind this barnyard fable. And so, even though there clearly exists an alternative conclusion that stops our story in its tracks, that leaves our all-too-imperfect Deity **forever** exercising his Eternal will-power---tho' it be in the seemingly superficial act of taking a never-changing, never-ending drink---, we shall not take that path. It does not satisfy us, even if it satisfy itself (as it does).

No, we would exhaust our God; we would project our own limits onto him. Or we would conclude that even an idealized, inexhaustible will-power may not be allowed to carry all before it: it may not feel free to cancel any alternative future save its own.

And it's even possible that the inevitable be accomplished WITHOUT narrative superimposition. Might there not be somewhat in Thor's character that would **desire** continuation even at the expense of his hallmark characteristic? Emergent now, at crisis-time?

Howsoever, Thor stopped that the story might go on. *Perpetuum mobile?*: not bloody likely! And, sure enough, a doubling-back took place: as when Thialfi entered the space-frame of his racing rival, Thor's defeat called out stony silence from both the Gigantic hosts and from their Host-of-hosts. And, as with Thialfi's efforts, 'twas the third time that charmed....

(24)

But silence was also made to be broken. "Oh, let's all drop pretence!" Utgard-Loki spat out, condescending to a non-Dramatic context. "Never believe that Giantism is *wholly* heartless. Observe, Thor, that we willingly move to thine own preferred level of discourse, narratively re-doubly-dundant. There! We're all back-stage, now, no longer captive to our roles. ...You are here to check us out and we're merely returning the compliment."

"But, in reality---", Loki began.

"---Pardon," Utgard-Loki interrupted, "but I confine my commentary to the ears of your full-blooded brother...and our Reader, of course. Yes, I'll happily confess my prejudicial disdain for the miscegenational likes of thee, Trick Baby. Oh, I know, I know: in some accounts your mother wasn't a Giant, so, like the Ortho-Doxies, you don't feel bound to identify with your tribe. But for us, that sinks you even lower! [Shudder of repulsion] ...Now, then, Thor, do you not find yourself increasingly comfortable in our company?"

The God, unwontedly reflective (seeking nobility in defeat?, finding it?) found himself incapable of reply.

"No? No matter," said Utgard-Loki. "In time, in time. We would learn of each other, right? So, let us pass on to one of the many ways Giants amuse themselves when left to their own devices. Attendants: bring forth my house-cat."

And, with that, a large black animal---furry, yes, but only vaguely feline---was urged into the hall. Its size dwarfed our entire company of heroes.

"This is Trouble, as I call her," the Hidden Head explained, "...or him? I've never really checked. But it has yet to reproduce, so who knows? And who really cares? You'll find us intolerant of such superficial distinctions: on one level, an indication of tolerance, don't you agree?"

Thor remained mute.

"Ah, well; to the business of pleasure! We Giants often delight the idle hour," said Utgard-Loki, "by dancing with Trouble. But of course she must first be set back on her hind legs; once that's accomplished, her endless tail will provide far more than the balance necessary to sustain a stately minuet or, if you're more that way inclined, a rollicking Mash' Potato. Lift 'er by the forepaws, Pardner! Let's have a pass-the-ducks!!"

Thor surveyed the creature before him.   An extravagant memory freaked through his mind but, before the God could name it, its place was taken by another memory, a memory not even his own but that of his superimpository Narrator; to wit: the image of the Narrator's two cats as doughty kittens, leaping at each other and clasping hooked paws in mid-air in a maneuver known   in   staged-wrestling   circles   as   the   Flying   Mare. Encouraged by this (as an emblem of the impossibly possible) and undeterred by the image's alien provenance [Who, after all, would claim that **all** our thoughts stem from one's own lived-experience   or   even   from   his   reading?],   Thor   grasped   the gargantuan, earth-hugging animal and attempted to heft him. Her?

Several mighty, mighty grunts succeeded in the lifting of one huge paw. Holding it over his head---for the longest time [Put a fermata on the score, here!]---, Thor was utterly stumped as to how further to proceed. This were no dance, he knew; not yet. Finally, he came upon the make-shift of working his way up the paw to the main body of the creature.   This painstaking, incremental procedure---which met with early, partial success--- caused something quite odd to happen: all of a sudden, the entire space-frame seemed tilted on edge [And who knew it had an edge?]; the chamber in which our chapter is set swept into a Gigantic panic, with behemoths falling all over each other and grabbing at the   heavy   stone   furniture,   desperately   seeking purchase; Loki and the Humes flattened out on the flagstone floor,   clinging   to   its   leaded   grooves;   Utgard-Loki   himself seemingly poised to topple off his throne (in fact, the observant Reader [the imaginative one, I mean] may even descry, for the first time, the Master-Monster's horrid mouth as it dropped, briefly, into the range of visibility; and, believe me, it were twisted into one ugly snarl!

This harum-scarum went on for some little time. In fact, spatial sanity was only restored when Thor, by now no stranger to defeat, realized that each advance up Grimalkin's paw was purchased at a definitive cost to his own vital sinew; in this, his second (and more direct) intimation of mortality, it was borne in upon the God that he could continue to lift the cat...or he could continue to live. So he dropped what he held. And automagically the Reality Twins, Space 'n' Time, righted themselves. Had something gone out of joint?, or whack?; Thor hadn't noticed: such was his total concentration. But über-Gigantic sighs of relief resounded throughout the chamber. And Utgard-Loki's pursed lips resumed, presumably, their place in the flies. There was a break in the action, as the G-of-G's retook his *amour propre*. At last, he said (with unexpected grimness): "We do have one *actual* trial to put you through, Thunder-maker. ...One assumes you can rassle?"

(25)

Thor nodded. Our God felt oddly buoyed; there's no clarity like confusion and confusion ain't no clarity at all. But there's an alternative node to the story-line here, Schnorri notes. In fact, there are two.

Yes, in one telling, it is Thor's sudden memory of his *only relative* immortality that lifts him up, compels him to make the most of his moment (even if it fall on the day before his eponymous "day"), renders him ready for anything!

And, in a third version (only newly conceived and immediately worshipped in the post-Modern Drama departments of what are still grandly called "universities"), Thor's choosing to drop Trouble's paw---choosing to live---fills our God not with Russell Hoban's "on-with" but with an unbearable despair.   At this critical junkstore, at this crippled/woebegone crux, Loki steps behind his half-brother and whispers in his left ear: "Thor, live tomorrow today," and then retreats into his handsome, clever, treacherous indignity. ...How does it happen that Thor's new-found life-anxiety [That's a translation from the Icelandic]---born of choice, of affirmation!--- is thereby resolved to a resplendent tranquility?:   how? This narrative-strain strains not to explain itself but simply describes: Thor absorbed the word from the guy who put the reason in treason, from his eventual betrayer, and found his lethargic mind thinking along the following lines: 'I **know** I'm real and that all this is really happening. No, I'm not a character in someone else's imagination. But it is *as if* I am!!' Perhaps it was this liberating, if inaccurate, perception that brought our hero-of-heroes back to his surface yet again, back to his Divine superficiality. Or maybe the God simply realized that he was *needed?*

Take your pick, Reader. All we know is this: when he heard Utgard-Loki float the notion of a rasslin' match, Thor licked his chops! 'Bring it on!!' he thought, echoing himself.

(26)

What got brought on was not the champion-of-champions the God expected to grapple with, no, but in his head that didn't really matter. It was tomorrow already [We swing with the third strain]; it was Thursday and Thor meant to live it through.

With what by now seemed to the protagonist a tiresome dissemblage, Utgard-Loki had declared a puzzled sympathy "in the light of our guest's clearly-performed incapacity to deserve his gaudy rep". Who would rassle Thor? was the question. No Giant "of any age" was unkind enough, enough the brute!, to agree to such an uneven match: "I regret to say, my dear Thor, that the least of these would wipe the floor with thee."

Thor, momentarily beyond anger, had kept his own counsel. The phrase "of any age" struck him funny; for, in looking about him, he saw only Giants that seemed to be of one and the same age! He'd heard recent mention of Giant toddlers but none was in evidence. Oh, well, they might be asleep or doing day-care; but there weren't any in-betweeners either. 'Perhaps, like some insects, they reach maturity then hew to the one basic form,' as I would tart up his musings. [He *did* flash on insects.] He'd also noted the absence of women. 'Keep 'em in purdah, maybe,' he'd thought.

But then a woman of sorts did appear: a crone, ancient beyond telling 'and little bigger than our human friends here', Thor observed. However, although he was evidently meant to be insulted by the match-up, our Deity was rather certain this lady would prove a formidable opponent.

"Here's Elli, my wet-nurse," said a formally-condescending Utgard-Loki. "She's willing to take you on."

Thor was right.

(27)

Herself proved a sublimely defensive fighter, conceding the God's every move, his every thrust, seeming to encourage them, to encourage *him*. Over and over, Thor thought he had the woman pinned, only to discover that the better part of her had somehow oozed out of his grip and was, in fact, *above* him, weighing him down. Had he ever gone outside his Western sphere, Thor might have recognized the techniques of Taoist rasslin' he had now to contend with; and, of course, he hadn't so he didn't. But Loki did.

"Give in!!" he shouted from the sidelines. "Stop trying to master her. Give in, it's your only chance, Thor. Lose yourself in her!"

And, for a second time, Loki's counsel was heeded...and met with narratively-utile results! Not that Thor ever gained the upper hand, no; but as the contest continued, as the God worked to surrender more and more of himself to it [Such that visual depictions of this agon tend not to discriminate between its combatants, tending instead to the non-figurative, to what I'd call "abstract expressionism" if that term didn't already possess a meaning of sorts], a restlessness set in among the Giant horde, a deafening stir that seemed directed upward, a roiling appeal to its head-hidden leader; and, in time, and not before time, himself felt compelled to act:

"All right. All right. Enough of that!" Utgard-Loki yelled/whispered. "I officially declare this match a draw!"

And that seemed somewhat to placate the near-rebellious Giant masses, who then settled into a murmuring discontent, still plenty loud by human standards. Loki, at this point, signed to Thialfi and Roskva that they must all three reach into the indistinct blur, get some blind purchase on Thor, and pull him out.

"He'll be the only solid object your hands will run across, so when they meet matter, grab and yank!" commanded our Trickster.

Significantly—at least to future denizens of Ultima Thule (a "living" theater), it was Roskva who, feeling for the helplessly-involved God, finally found him. Not Loki, hip to the narrative necessity of his brother's discovery; not Thialfi, already projected by futurian marketeers as the fleet, blond troll-model who'd draw teeming draughts of human teens to the holographic rendition of our wintry tale. No, it was none other than that forgotten, hitherto unlimned, all-but-anonymous errata-slip of a girl...the why of which will be ultimately obvious. [Oh well, she'll be in the holomovie too, as I've already projected]

For now, I'll say (with Schnorri) that Roskva knew the flesh of others when she felt it, while the males kept coming up with themselves.

"She has him!" Loki cried and he and the girl's brother fastened their hands onto what hers held and pulled and pulled until the blob came far enough into their world—our world!—that recognizable features could no longer be denied. It was their Thor, our Thor, right as rain; stunned, silent, but Thor.

He proved himself himself when consciousness finally dawned and he realized his presence in the life-saving [How else to put it?] embrace of two humans [Bad Karma!] and his trustably-untrustable brother [Bad form!!]. Thor was quite unused to being rescued at all and, in short, he was embarrassed.

"Okay: back off, all of you!" he bleated, gruffly; Gods are seldom grateful.

Elli, meanwhile, had worked her own self into distinction---unaided---and withdrew into the room's roomy shadows.

Does the Reader see in all this something of a breather? She may. But Utgard-Loki knew that the situation was, in fact, highly sensitive, febrile, a crux; order and chaos equally-likely; so he seized the moment before either destiny could play its hand:

"That's it for show 'n' tell," he declared. "We Giants have hammered into your brain-pans just who we are. And you Gods...well, Jotenheim has a far clearer picture of you, now. And of your slaves, come to that. So let's eschew all notions of comparison and do what all three of our species do so very well: let's eat!!!"

(28)

And so, with his jerked-out, massive brachials flashing obscure signals ('Looks like *tai-chi* on chrystal-meth,' Loki mused), Utgard-Loki, Jint of Jints, called into being the following: an ever-changing olfactory blend of all that awakens hunger in all who allow themselves to feel it; and a radical transformation in the huge room's mood-lighting from primary austerity to pastel *Gemütlichkeit;* and an o'er-whelming, segmental wooden-device---coextensive with the room itself---, the moving metal joints of which were soon observed to be herding the room's occupants each into his own little six-sided confinement---with room to stand, yes, certainly room to respire, but little more; one could apply torsion to torso, for example, but no one could step out of line nor cast his gaze below his own abdomen: "We are en-isled," as Loki acknowledged, aloud. "We're locked into our lives. Hmm...." Yet this odd process of mechanistic individuation was met by a stultifyingly jovial shout from the Giant masses, who'd evidently been through it all countless times and loved it!

As each organic entity was thus corralled, the act was followed by a thick metallic *click!*, a sound somehow deeply-satisfying to a Frost- or Mountain Giant [Schnorri never makes clear which we are dealing with, here]; yes, each click was met with a massive sigh of pleasure. A room of one's own, to be sure, with literal elbow-room the one amenity.

All four of our wayfarers were, *heureusement*, within eye-shot of each other. Thor---as yet a sight uncomfortable within his own singular mold (*i.e.*, still unused to being simply himself again (("Lost myself back there, didn't I?" he said, but too softly for anyone else to hear.))---was just cautiously regarding the vaguely hexagonal shape of the opening that had closed about his midsection when, all of a sudden, an unseen bit of chair-like clockwork struck him smartly behind the knees, necessitating a sitting posture, his elbows crashing down on the roof of his cell. Thor looked about. All were in the same boat, so to speak, or in nearly identical crafts of the same make. Only nearly so, he noted, as some contrivance had leveled the size-disparity between human and God, between God and Giant.

"Yass, yass," Utgard-Loki crudely interrupted. "Everyone's chair brings him up to the same mark. Why?, you seem to wonder. Think, Man! We are all but sedentary creatures before the necessity of sustenance. Even you, Forrester. Especially you! Denial, here, serveth no purpose but its own. Oh, I know myself a higher being; and I identify with my own trip, don't get me wrong: let hierarchy reign!!...elsewhere. It will anyway. But not at table. No. Not at stool; nor at table. There...and there: all are meek before the Untouchable Deities of Continuity: Repletion and her mate, Elimination."

With this, thankfully, Utgard-Loki ceased his shpiel. And, as he did so, viands beyond description descended upon what was indeed---as Thor dully noted---the extended table that was each entity's durance vile.

Loki glanced at his miserable brother and said, "'Enjoy, oh, enjoy your suffering', so say all your Western mystics. Dig in, Thor!"

[Your Narrator must now excuse himself to dine. He suggests his Reader follow suit.]

(29)

All within the Throne Room ate and ate. Loki, ordinarily the soul of appetite, found, for a change, his hunger matched by everyone else's. Indeed, in a rare moment between bites, when the Surpriser threw his gaze aloft, hoping to steal a glance at Utgard's massive regent, he saw to his wild surmise that You-Ell himself had had his motion as tabled as anyone in the room; 'Even he finds himself confined,' Loki registered, 'if on a grander scale.' His Trickery watched in some awe as the outsize arms of the Jint-of-Jints scooped up---in continuous, windmill fashion---the constantly-replenished fare set before him, food destined to disappear into the rough cloud enveloping that hidden head. Loki sighed and returned to his own ever-filled plate.

Yes!, God and Giant and human all ate as if their lives depended on it. And then, as if in furtherance of that observation, as if in subjunctive tribute to the flimsiness of continued existence, the food chain came unlinked. All that provender came to an abrupt end. Next, the tables themselves fell away; a general huzzah went up as wiggle-room was, at last, provided for all present.

Then the participants felt something nudging their feet: each entity was being offered his/her own personal platform.

"Step on it!" ordered Utgard-Loki in his booming whisper.

"Best comply," counseled our own Loki.

Sound advice!, as the floor immediately fell away [As in THE ROTOR, an amusement-park ride from the Narrator's youth].

"A post-prandial piss is warmly suggested," suggested You-Ell, warmly enough.

The resultant sizzle had the sonic force of the entire Disco Era compressed into one blatant moment. [Would that it had been, in Reality!, say I.]

"Dribble and shake," the Boss ordered, channeling the caller at an Appalachian square-dance.

There was general obedience, Roskva practicing the rite in her own way. Then all Giant eyes were seen to turn upward, happy anticipation written on the weathered, uncannily similar faces. Irresistibly our Gods and humans joined their gaze. What they saw---greeted again by cheers from the room at large ---was the erratic, wafting descent of dozens of silky, golden feathers. Then dozens more, met with ever-noisier acclaim. Finally, whole rafts of the stuff---true software!---tumbled out of the flies. These proved purposeful (programmed?) quills which bonded with each other once they reached the ground, forming an ultra-cushy, lateral/literal featherbed, occupying the Throne Room entire. As if on cue, lights were doused and, in a flash, a pure darkness plunged over all.

"And so to bed," peeped Utgard-Loki and our people, pooped, were delighted to obey.

(30)

SCHNNORRI: Zz!

(31)

But before sleep could put its needles to the raveled sleeve of care, a brief colloquy-under-arms took place between our Divine half-brothers.

LOKI: They *have* us, you know.

THOR: All too well.

LOKI: **And** we've been had! ... But you know---for the life of me, Dunder!!---I can't parse the distinction between the two! I fail to see any difference, you dig?

With that, the Trickster began to giggle---an insane, relentless giggling, long and hard.

Something in Thor snapped. His hands formed fists; he growled, low in his gut.

And Loki's giggle continued, coming and going in spasms. Thor found himself thinking, 'It's like the fire in the Giant's glove: all but put out, only to flare up elsewhere.' Grimly, our principal protag resolved to wait it out. Had you been there, my Reader, you'd find self treated to a cantata of giggles punctuated by low growls: celestial scoring by the ghost of Conlon Nancarrow, denied his true instrument: no player-pianos in Heaven!; indeed, no machines of any sort.

Yet---and may you never tire of hearing this repeated!---everything this side of the Divide (shades of the Divine!) must come to an end. When the giggling at last went extinct, Thor spoke: "Loki...I fail to find any humor in your failure to make that distinction: have, had, or what-have-you. Nor in our situation as a whole. We've been shown up, literally belittled...and they have us right where they want us. T'ain't funny."

Loki called out into the darkness, "Thialfi, human proto-hero, would-be speed demon, art thou near-by?"

"Aye, Sir," said the lad, "although just the near-side of sleep."

"Hark unto me for half-a-tick, then we'll all surrender to the undertow of what the Moderns will misidentify as the 'Unconscious'. ...But in so saying, I'm dating myself, aren't I?, as the amorous solipsist put it."

Loki began to cackle. Thor grunted. Whilst, all about our wan party, nocturnal noises came to the fore, as one Giant after another dropped off to Dreamland.

"I'd *like* to laugh about what's happened, what's happening," Thialfi owned.

"Oh, you'll get the joke in time, see the point," Loki assured him. "You and your kind will come to see that all possession is imaginary. But not yet. No, not yet."

Thor re-grunted.

"You see, my brother here is fundamentally humorless," Loki said. "And it's because he knows no fear."

"But they have us, as I heard you say," said Thialfi. "Yet you yourself are not afraid, either."

"I?" said Loki. "I am all fear, Lad."

"I couldn't tell," Thialfi said. "It doesn't show."

"That-a-boy!" Loki said. "Yes, I'm all about appearance: 'tis, I realize,the Giant in me. But I'm as proud of my fear as I am of what masks it!"

"But why? My own fear shames me."

"Only because you have yet to learn," Loki said, "how to use it as a source of concentration."

"Concentration on **what?**, I'd like to know!" Thor put in, rudely.

"Concentration on what's imaginary, my Dear: a field *you* will never fear to tread."

Thor grunted yet again.

"Can you make it clearer to me?" Thialfi wished to know.

"I've no desire to," Loki said, airily. "But I *will* tell you this: only through the screen of the imagination will you humans eventually see death for what it is. ...Oh, eventually!"

"Perhaps I need a new master," Thialfi suggested.

"Master yourself!" Loki snapped. "Elsewise, you don't stand a chance."

"Listen to him," commanded Roskva (*sans* irony), her first recorded words.

"I would hope that---" Thialfi began.

"No!" said Loki; then added, more gently, "No. There's no *hope*, in any case; not for you: you're mortal. Take it from a mythomaniac, Kid."

"Pipe down!!" Thor shouted. A tense silence ensued.

But Loki, all nerve/nerves, couldn't contain himself (*i.e.,* spilling over in fear that he be spilt). "Thor?" he asked, stiff moments later.

"Well?"

"They've been nice to us, here at the literal end-of-the-day: feeding us, tucking us in, treating us as if *we* were no different from *them*: being nice."

"Yeah, I know: it's worse."

"You reckon?"

"Victors can be generous."

"Or tolerant? Like the Moslems, classically, when they take control?"

"I wouldn't know," Thor said. "That hasn't happened yet, right?"

"Right," Loki conceded.

"But I'm in a hell-of-a-fix in my head when I can't even grouse with impunity! Crikey!, I find I can't *hate* these motherfuckers. Is that any way to regard an enemy?! ...Oh, well, fuck it!: I can't even concentrate on my discomfort. I don't even *feel* any discomfort; they've taken that away, even that! Fuck it; let's go to sleep, Loki. Maybe tomorrow, even if it won't be *my* day, any longer.... Maybe, I'll feel more like myself, come tomorrow. As you say, 'This were sometime a conundrum,' eh, Loki? ...Loki?"

But Thor's final address was declaimed into a void, a noisy void, filled to the gills with the nocturnal irruptions of a huge host of hyperstertorous slumberers, including one temporally-liberated trickster, two brave youngsters, and a Giant horde with its overmastering commander. And, soon enough, a disappointed God would join the same chorus.

And the Throne Room---which, although commodious, was in Reality only a species of commode, a setting for the elimination-round of a far grander contest---nonetheless mocked its future, becoming transformed into a vast sphere, a cathedral of dreams , a cathexis in its narthex ("A bloomin' advert fer Sominex!" as Loki quipped...from wherever he was, keenly conscious of his temporary mock-stasis within *our* context. Remember: he doesn't dream.)

And, along with these our characters, Reader, we must add in an aging Narrator, down to his last pack of lies (*Mensonges,* unfiltered). Yes, and behind it all, and no less unconscious for that, an ancient fabulist who probably never lived and will doubtless never die. Yes, my Reader, we have come, at last, to a coincidence of zzz's.

(32)

SCHNORRI: Z!

(33)

To me, Schnorri proves his daft loyalty to his kind (ours?) by not permitting any Modern inspection of whatever flickering cinema played before the nether attention of his characters on this particular night. 'Let 'em snooze!' appears to be his unrecorded attitude. Yes, graced by the bestowal of a writerly parody of "private life", all screens went blank for hours and hours and hours on end. (Although I do find it provocative that our Mr. Zzzz's ((non-possessive)) does *not* seem privy to Utgard-Loki's inner life, duzzy?)

As with so much observed within the tale, this general oblivion betokens a more heroic era than my Late Modernity or your half-fledged Age of Drama, Reader. But desire cuts cross time zones, agreed? What better means to draw humans and their Projections to waking consciousness than the blissed-out aroma of a blest breakfast?! Yes, yes, Speedy Reader, I know: to you, these folk just dined, mere pages ago. But for them, the period between chapters is a species of hibernation and the recurrence of appetite the point. ...As I say: more heroic.

But even ample rest will not resolve the emotional lump 'neath the physical coverlet. Unwelcome gratitude sat on Thor's tummy all through the night and even as the God woke up and smelled the coffee (which came first?), it sat there still. Appetite won out, of course; it always does; but even as the Thunderer wolfed down his massive portion of the dainties set before the company as a whole (with the food literally dumped into each lap), his inner man found something stuck in his craw: 'WHY?, after my inconclusive rassle with that old lady, did this rum crew turn so grandly hospitable? Why make nice with critters like us, so clearly so far down the phylogenetic scale?'

He looked around. The human kids seemed unbothered by any such doubts; they were up and gobbling greedily. Loki, too; his face was buried in his plate.

Thor re-cast his gaze onto the head-shrouded headman of Utgard, doing so just in time to see his sometime nemesis bring meaty palms together in a mighty clap-slap. This signal brought about an unwonted result: all the Giants, save their leader, dropped what they were eating or guzzling: actually "dropped" it, as plates and goblets and harmware clattered to the floor, 'a floor miraculously free of feathers,' as Thor only now noticed.

Utgard-Loki clapped a second time and this wrought an even weirder change: throughout the room, all Giants (but one) threw themselves down and immediately set about to arranging their bodies crosswise on the bare flagged-out floor, the effect resembling a series of rough tangents, such that the head of each Giant lay comfortably on the abdomen of his neighbor. After the entire body (the exception proving the cliché) was so arranged, its components, with one will, fell back to sleep.

Our party looked all about them, amazed; in the animated-cartoon version of the story---rivalling in popularity, as it eventually would, the interactive Hologram Movie (shamelessly entitled "Be Thor Now!")---a vast, pulsating thought-balloon floated over the gang of four, its tails extending one to each humanoid head, its common message: 'WHAT NEXT?'

Loki, wryly smiling, appeared just about to comment on this odd, Ontolovisual phenomenon. But Utgard-Loki pre-empted his shame-sake with a resounding third clap which, wondrous to relate, succeeded in jerking open the storied gates of Jotenheim. This action didn't exactly flood the scene with light: it **was** day, outside, but our Mr. Sun---fount of all encouragement---seemed to have gone into hiding. Somehow the to-be-expected distinction between inside and outside struck Thor, at least, as blurrier than it ought to have been.

Then...Utgard-Loki---in the booming insinuation they'd come to know so well---announced, "You are free to go."

"What can that mean?" Thor wondered/whispered to Loki: "That the demeaningly-defeated be permitted a safe, if ignominious, retreat?, that we remain alive to tell the tale...of the ruin yet to come?"

The half-bred Prank-King chuckled. "It's naught but ponderous, any time you set yourself to pondering, my dim brother! Yet it's also...touching."

"The fuck **is** happening, then?" Thor demanded.

"Take your cue from the visuals," Loki answered, gently. "You've likely noticed that the freedom we've just been offered uncannily resembles the captivity we've encountered?"

"Yeah, I clocked that. But I don't get it, Man."

"Sure you do," Loki said. "We're being reminded that, even as Gods, we're mortal in one sense: we can't get outside our lives until we die. But, look, Thor!---our human companions have stolen a march on us: they're half-way out the gate!"

"Then who are we to hang about? [Torn] ...On the other hand, why bother?"

But it was true enough! Roskva and Thialfi were taking turns urging each other forward, unencumbered by mythic complications, somehow intuiting that any distinctions between now and what was to come would have perforce to be forged within their own souls.

"'Forged'? That's accurate," Loki mocked. "When it comes to play-by-play, Reader, JF's a stone *homer*. Shades of KDKA's Bob Prince! ...Oh, don't mind me, Thurston; talking to myself. Let's catch up with the kids; join 'em in the Great Sameness."

And the two dispirited Deities trudged toward an opening each held to be essentially arbitrary: with waking-life a lifeless parody of nightmare, how can difference make a difference?

"One moment, You Two!" Utgard-Loki commanded.

The Gods froze, turned to face the source of the voice...only to find the throne unoccupied! Thor and Loki looked at each other, then back at the emptiness. But they would not be left long in astonishment; no, the disembodied voice would soon return---once again Dramatic, replete with explanation, and reeking with Gigantic "sincerity".

UTGARD-LOKI: I'm just practicing a little ventriloquism, Guys. Picked up that skill from Schnorri Hisselves! Yeah, I'm actually outside, myself; I'm just throwing my voice back in. Doing so, in order to urge you to join me out here. [Cue semi-mental strings] I know the future doesn't strike either of you'uns as any too bright. ...But I gotta come clean about a few things. Level with you. 'N' that's best face-to-face, right? Also, I really must give you both a proper send-off!

LOKI: Thor?

THOR (gritting his massive molars): Actually, I feel we have no choice. Let's go.

LOKI (with a pretense of indifference; yet actually *meaning* it?): Yeah, later with this scene.

(34)

But the world outside, despite its drab visuals, held a fine---if abrupt---surprise for our jaded Gods. Some distance off, they beheld the suddenly towering presence of their two pet humans, flanking a rather large, rather familiar figure; holding converse with him.

Loki was briefly charmed. "Look at that, Thor!" he exclaimed: "Our kids have sprouted up! And who's that with them? Why...it looks like our one-time tour-guide, Skrymir. He, on the other hand, appears...somewhat diminished."

"More Gigantic perceptual chicanery," Thor groused, his vocabulary---his mental acuity!---blossoming in the gloom. "We ought to be used to it by now. Yes, I reckon if we walk toward them, our perspective will condense. Same-old same-old. The humans'll shrink to their proper size. About the big lug, I don't know: he may be an independent variable."

"Thor, what's come over you?" Loki fretted. "Got into you?"

But the two were soon within earshot and found themselves greeted by what was, indeed, their erstwhile guide.

"Welcome, Gents, welcome," said the Giant. [Imagine him voiced by a 50s game-show host] "Welcome to the ex-urbs of Utgard. And---you're right, Hammerman!---I am, in Reality, not that much larger than you chaps. More hulking, certainly. More nightmare beast from the human unconscious than the Beatified projection of an ego-ideal."

"Point taken, Skrymer," said Loki, "and it's good to see the kids once again no bigger than their britches."

"But he's *not* Screamer!" Thialfi piped up.

"Well, yes and no," the Giant agreed and disagreed. "As I was just explaining to your bright youngsters, here, the name I might most accurately answer to...is Utgard-Loki. Yes. In my Throne Room---in recent chapters past---, had my head not been veiled, you'd have noted the resemblance."

"A splendid put-on," Loki offered, in frank admiration.

But Thor was pissed. "Don't you see?" he half-yelled at his half-brother. "This is the **ultimate** in their belittlement of us: they reduce themselves to our size, *yet* they dominate!! Let's go home."

UTGARD-LOKI (on his high horse): Not so fast, Big Guy. Ain't you at all interested in the truth?

THOR (with a gruesome growl): "Truth"? What's that?

LOKI (chuckling heartily): As if this were a Passion Play! Aye, Thor: just now, there's more to thee than passes show!

U-L: What is truth? Why, what it always is/are: whatever permits life to change, or, whatever points up change as the only Reality. Didn't you catch our opening number?

THOR: All right. But I don't particularly dig this run of changes, one deceptive cadence after another; how's a bebopper s'posed to blow on 'em?, let alone do the *collective* number, like old Nawlins or late- 60s New Yawk? **And** the time is out of joint!!

LOKI: My Man, you are *all over the place*, all at once! Hmm...hmm....

THOR: Now...you feed us, you free us, you jolly us along. I think you were "truer" before you changed. I preferred you huge, headless, and openly nasty. ...Just give us leave to wander on home, lick our wounds in Asgard. I, for one, know when I'm in the presence of my betters. I just *forgot* for a hot minute. ...C'mon Loki, Kids: we've a helluva trudge ahead of us. *That* we know.

[Thor turns away]

U-L: Contradictory being!! How can one creature be so strong and yet at once so wrong!?

LOKI: He can't help it, Yul. The two qualities go hand-in-hand.

U-L: Well, yes, they do. And this topples every hierarchy, given time. ...Notwithstanding your Bard's undue respect for rank, for degree. Of course, his lunatics are well-aware of this, be they kings, fools, or suicides.

LOKI: Not *our* Bard. And too far afield, Yuletide. You'll only addle the lad further. Thor's got...integrity issues, just now. Picking up signals from too many sources.

[The Thunderer, who had indeed turned to go, stops irresolutely]

(35)

U-L (gently): Thor, you may believe me or not, as you are capable. But listen: we fed you...because we **feared** you. Feared all of you, the least of you: the least the most, in fact.... Now that you are outside the walls of Utgard, I may safely say these things, risk honesty. And, trust me, had I had a tinkling inkling of your destructive might, you would *never ever* have been permitted inside, never within striking distance of my throne, of my being: the memory of it quakes me!

LOKI: How can these things be?

U-L: I am no bigger than you see me now, nor ever was. No, the only muscles we Giants flexed, throughout your scouting mission, were the sinews of our gray matter: our ability to flummox. And, even then, we needed constantly to have our wits about us. No, we fed you...lest in your raging hunger you might decide to consume us all! You, Loki, set that fear in us. Yikes!

LOKI: My brother wants convincing.

U-L: Thor, regard that grand canyon directly in front of you.

THOR: Yeah, what about it?

U-L: You don't remember it, do you? It wasn't there before, was it?

THOR: No. No it wasn't. So?

U-L: But it was. And you're the force responsible for it. It's *your* ditch, Deity.

THOR (surveying the vast hole-in-the-ground, miles across): Geologic fissures over untold millennia? Shift in the techtonic plates, explained mythically?

U-L: You **don't** know what you're talking about.

THOR: No. Those are just words I've heard. From somewhere. Maybe from *him.* [Jerks thumb over right shoulder, indicating Loki; continues to stare into the hole]

U-L: Okay, here's the real deal, although I warn you you won't like it.

THOR: Don't like much of anything, just now. Tell me.

U-L: Dig it: the massive ground-gap at your feet is the pure product of that third mighty swipe you took at my forehead. Remember that? You put some oomph behind that throw, Bro!

THOR: What I remember is that it affected you not at all.

U-L: Not physically, no. But it was my emotional introduction to your...pronounced formidability.

THOR: Can the flattery. If my hammer-heave made that hole, how come I only see it now? And how did I miss the target? I *was* aiming for your left temple.

U-L: Oh, your aim was unerring. Your problem was: I wasn't there! No, your *first* toss had scared the bejeebers outa me---I saw it coming and rolled away **just** in time. Truth to tell, Thor, that initial heave was your only real shot at a premature ending to this tale. Thereafter, I took pains to live among you folk *strictly through images.* Like Ulysses among the women?

THOR (with barely-suppressed fury): So...it's likely that you're not even here, right now.

U-L: Likely not, no. For us Giants, negative space is malleable. We just slap some on, whenever there's aught we want to cover up. The illusion dissolves with its need. For example, when you continue on, the way you're facing, you'll come across those two large glens indicative of hammer-tosses one and two.

LOKI: Tell us what you mean by "images" and the whole thing will come clearer.

U-L: Well, for example, Prankster, the reason your muscle-man couldn't open my wallet---to get the food out?---was because I'd bound it with five impossibilities: a concept you Aesir will yourselves employ...to bind one of my eventual allies, one of your righteous offspring, Loki: the Fenris wolf.

[Reader: check out *that* story in Schnorri]

LOKI: Ah. Images, you're saying, as situational representations---

U-L: ---belong to no one, no. I used another story---or another part of the same story---to hide from you. Ventriloquism and image-projection: these are the skills of Giantism.

THIALFI: Back up! How can anything be both fictional and impossible?

U-L: What I meant about all of you being dangerous to us! No, you're quite right, Son. Things are only impossible when they fly in the face of the agreed-upon meaning of the terms you use. When they defy language.

THOR: Hoity toity! Humpty Dumpty! There **must** be something beyond games, deeper than games.

LOKI: A whole world, my brave Know-Nothing!

THIALFI (to Utgard-Loki): Something in me needs for you to spell it out, Sir. To provide examples for a mind that apprehends through distinctions...or thinks it does. What did you use to make us see things awry?

U-L: Oh, from Schnorri's horde, I culled the footfall of a cat and the spittle of a bird. From future sources, I unearthed the soul of your approaching Singularity: I know ALL about that, first-hand! And from Forrester's present, the way to oppose an enemy without coming to resemble him.

LOKI: That's four.

(36)

[Thor turns turk]

THOR (to Utgard-Loki): And all that went down within the gates of your city: that was all hooey, as well?

U-L (defensively): Defensive illusion. We used what we had ---and who we are---to protect ourselves. Even then, things got mighty dicey, all too often. You couldn't bend the bars of our gate because they were made up of the shortest distance between two points, replicated over and over. And its rod was forged of Lifelong Disappointment. Had those illusions come undone, both outer- and inner-Reality would have to be re-drawn.

LOKI: This I find fascinating! When I entered the eating contest---

U-L: ---Oh, yes: that! You may have noticed that all flavor went away, soon after you dug in.

LOKI: Actually, I didn't. My prodigious appetite tends to feed off itself.

U-L: Yes and when we realized that, we substituted inorganic material for the original content of your trough: anyone else would have found it scarcely edible. Frankly, we feared the depletion of our kitchen supplies!

LOKI: And yet your guy still won the contest.

U-L: Yes and that's because he wasn't a humanoid of any sort. You would've out-eaten any Giant on the set, Loki.

LOKI: Thanks for that. But what *was* he, then?

U-L: Well, like you Gods and you humans, we Giants have fire. Humans keep warm and cook food with it; Gods require it for rituals. Giants---following our own needs and predilections---, we *personify* it. We give fire a form and it dwells within our commune as an equal. You were pitted against fire, Loki. Little wonder you lost. Fire doesn't discriminate! ...Oh, well, it does, of course. But we figgered that a wooden trough'd be the most historically-apposite grub-repository. Haulin' big chunks o' stone in would slow down the story 'n' plastic ain't been invented as yet. You ate what was in the trough because it looked like food. Hugi consumed the trough itself because nobody told him not to. Because nobody stopped him. As in the Harmonica Blow, Clinton's defense?: because he *could*.

THIALFI: And my race? Was that rigged, as well?

U-L: In a way, Son.

THIALFI (hardening):   In the same way?, through personification? Did you pit me against some other aspect of fire?

U-L: It might be read that way.

THOR: Come on! Level with the kid!!

U-L: I'm trying, Thor. I am. But you will ALL have to understand that a lifetime of perfecting duplicity, of dissimulation---of working to create an impression?---has left me, when honesty is called for, at something of a loss. The truth is not in me.

LOKI: Half of my being can sympathize with that, Yule-log.... While the other half is righteously indignant.

ROSKVA: Say what you will say, Giant. We'll determine how much we believe.

[Simultaneously:]

THOR (amazed): Ooooo!

LOKI (*sotto voce*): Jesus.

THIALFI (proudly): Wow!!!

(37)

UTGARD-LOKI (dropping pretense with a thud): Very well. ...And the girl is right: I could care less about any of you. [To Thialfi:] You ran not against fire, Boy, but against one of its referential equivalents: Successive Time. He too / She too / It too...has a place at our table.

THIALFI (with scorn): Your imaginary table.

U-L: Just so.

LOKI: Dig the kids, Thor!

U-L: And a wave of fear broke over us---we Giants, I mean---when you forced us to behold actual humanity and abstract Time---in motion---within the same visual frame. Fortunately, for all concerned, this took place near the end of your race. You glimpsed the moving image of Eternity, Young Man. Or its hind quarters, anyway. Had the moment been sustained, we none of us would be here now.

THOR (sourly): What's so special about that?

LOKI: Hush, Brother. How often do we get our illusions dispelled?

U-L: Inexorable Time! He can be a ruthless dinner companion, let me assure you. And as a jogging partner!!!: each step he takes brings death that much closer. You ran the course three times, Lad. Each time the victor crossed the finish line, he rehearsed what lies in wait...for you, for us, for all who vie with Time.

SCHNORRI (waking up with a start, a snort; crabby old voice): But Forrester is in error here!! My annals clearly indicate that Thialfi races not against "Sucessive Time"---whatever that is!---, but against "thought" itself...which, of course, takes no time.

U-L: Not "thought", ancient Codger-slash-Dodger. *My* thought! And my thought *is* Time. Chronos is one of my eponyms. Look it up.

SCHNORRI: My quarrel's not with you, Character, but with your Po-Mo Narrator. [To Forrester:] Do you claim to draw from some deeper well?, some more authentic source than my hard-won prose 'n' poesy?

NARRATOR: Actually, *taking thought* is what my manuscript purports to be about: my Daddy's beeswax.

SCHNORRI: Well, if that's your tiresome excuse for a memory-lapse, Forrester, I'm off to sleep again, if nobody minds.

THOR: There's that infernal buzzing again!!

LOKI: It's just old Schnorrer, keeping us dishonest...as if that were actually possible! He's for a jig or a poke, then he dozes. Tedious! [To Utgard-Loki:] Say on, Giant. Don't mind the inter-ructions.

UTGARD-LOKI: I don't, in either sense. And, in fact, I find confession sweet, if *un peu difficile*. [More gently:] Yes, well, if you-lot be willing to re-live your needless embarrassment, I'm willing to face down the terror we Giants felt as you dealt with our filigreed makeshifts in your own brutal way.

THOR: What "terror"?

U-L: Recall, Thor, the episode of the drinking horn?

THOR: All too readily.

U-L: What we hid from you---and from the Reader---was the link between that horn and the Thulean Sea.

THOR: It seemed to me a discrete item, the horn.

U-L: It would. Remember my skill at slapping on negative space at will. ...On your return journey to Asgard, cast your eyes seaward and see in amazement how much **land** your draughts reclaimed, a veritable Holland! Giants are humanoid but we are, in a sense, akin to brine-shrimp. Sent-away-for sea monkeys from the back pages of old comic-books? Our illusive form is naught without water. The ocean is our true home. ...Well, it is for humans too, but they've long forgotten that. So we Giants are environmentalists-by-necessity, not by Aristotelian choice. Your grand gulps diminished our water supply, Thor, robbed us of our mother's milk, attacked our origin without mercy if without intent. Naturally, we quailed. We thought the parody of the strap-on pisser would distract you---it imitated both the drinking horn and the drinker---but instinctively you spurned it. Ohhh, was I ever **glad** when you took that horn from your lips!!

(38)

LOKI: And the cat dance?

UTGARD-LOKI: Oh, yes! In that, I had to rely upon your brother's legendarily-slow thought-processes.

THOR: Now **that's** an attitude I recognize as authentically yours, Giant!

U-L: But it turns out our scouting reports were as exaggerated as those of Twain's death. Yes, Thor, you *almost* remembered what you were about. Had you done so, you'd have succeeded in undoing the world.

THOR: I have no such power.

U-L: But you do. In your first recorded feat, you bestowed integrity upon the orb whereon your humans dwell. ...Oh well, we Jints live there too---we're terrestrial---but we inhabit a dimension accessible only to the autistic and will remain incorporeal to humankind until autism's secrets are shared. ...But that's both by-the-way and, eventually, the point.

THOR: I know nothing of this feat.

U-L: No. The well-spring of your strength is your ignorance of the results of what you do; that's clear. But you may, Thor, have a dim memory of having bent the Midgard Serpent to your will.

LOKI: Um.

U-L: Yes, another of *your* creatures, Handsome. You bequeathed to it your ego...which dwells within the beast in an unobstructedly pure form. Its mouth is ever open: it is the Empowered Consumer beloved of late-Modern economies. Ego, of course, is necessary, Zen Westerns notwithstanding: it is productive of distinction, hence a child of consciousness---

LOKI: *Merci.*

U-L: ---but it must, itself, be distinct or all creation is forever at war. This were, ahem, "sometime a paradox" but you, Thor, answered it with your proto-Alexandrian crudity. You whipped that serpent around the globe, then jammed its tail into its gullet, rammed it deep, made of it a monstrous *Möbius* strip. Then you cast the whole critter into the darkest ocean of the human unconscious. As such, it holds the world together.

THOR (slowly but with growing pride): Yes, I am said to have done that.

U-L: And it will continue to provide integrity---to a world that would surely fall apart otherwise---until the serpent finally realize that it is itself it would consume, itself it would swallow. Then and only then will it rise, extend itself, and join forces with *my* kind, the creatures of imagination. Then and only then will we take on you Deities...or "human projections", as we think of you. But this warfare must **not** be prematurely waged. Not if it is to have meaning. Believe me, it were pointless, should Rognarok become no more than ***entertainment*** for future humans, if indeed there be any. Pointless, because *change* is ever the point!!

THOR: I don't yet---

U-L: ---No, of course not. Dig: my pet "cat"-in-quotes was, in Reality, co-extensive with the Midgard Serpent, that which you heroically subdued, back in your forgotten youth. Somewhat like Heracles, strangling the snakes in his cradle, but grander!, much grander.

LOKI: And when he lifted up its paw---

U-L: ---yes, when he did that, it stirred the memory of the creature---thy creature, Loki. It caught an inkling of its destiny...and it began to loosen its jaws. And your brother: he too began to remember his past---which were a presage of his limited future, should things go on the way they were.

LOKI: Had my slimy child's tail come loose---

U-L: ---it would have dissolved the Space/Time continuum, rent the coincidence that makes the moment possible, tore it irreparably, leaving existence with only a past and a future. That would not, could not have happened, not yet. But you saw what even a slight loosening produced: your whole frame went topsy-turvy. Oh, well, maybe you *didn't* see it, Thor. [He didn't]. As for me, I deemed it likely I'd be tossed off my throne.

Heureusement---for whatever reason---you, Thunderthud, found yourself unwilling to die. Not today. And, hence, saved us all!

THOR: To fight another day.

U-L: Yes.

[Narrative note: Actually, I substituted *my* memory for Thor's, at that critical moment. Not that I expect any Readerly credit for it.]

LOKI: Boo!!!

UTGARD-LOKI: Hissssss!!!

THOR: Huh? If that gnat once show itself, I'll **swat** the sucker, see if I don't!

(39)

THOR (seeing nothing, calming down; to Loki): Okay, what I want to know is: all this high-toned phoniness: howzicome you couldn't see through it, Trick-or-Treat?, you being aware of the script 'n' all?

LOKI: No, Bro. I'm only aware that there is a script. Oh, I see it...but only after it hits the page; and, in Life, that's still hindsight. Content is the great mystery, not form.

UTGARD-LOKI: And that, you'll find, has as much to do with everything as anything. And, incidentally, Guys: to your term "script" we Giants prefer "program". It's eventually far more accurate. I never let a "story" get in the way of a few hard facts! For example...I promise you, Thor, that you won't understand this, but the likes of you and Loki *and* the likes of me are, in Reality, little more than well-decorated dead-ends for the Beings who brought us forth.

THOR: And who may **they** be, when they're at home?

U-L: Why, humankind, of course. We're all in a tale. Can't you tell that you're being told?

LOKI: He can't. Curse of a strong character. ...But in what sense do we represent human failure?

U-L: In this: that the only failure worth the name is the failure to change. And *we* cannot change because we lack the temporal context: we don't age, haven't you noticed? Humans in hot pursuit of their fading youth will never recognize mortality as their ally, as their portal to change. No, they prefer to imitate you and me, identify with us, live a privileged pretense...until that grows stale, until they can't fool themselves any longer: Bored-again Believers, most of their lives. And forever at war.

LOKI: I grasp your point, Giant. As Gods, Thor and I are IDEAL, so I see how we are born to mislead. We offer a brief glimpse at suppressed grandeur, a concentration of humanity wholly unobtainable. Gods are Romantic, our moment the Chopin-hour, the world as willy-nilly gimmick. But what of you folk? You are more purely imaginary.

U-L: Ah, but we are not a *Volk*, we Giants. We are but one being. We are the monstrous foretelling of an engineered amalgam of the Terrans and their mechanisms. We have become one through the rigor of efficiency. Humankind? **You** would have them die of boredom. Their own egos would let them die of embarrassment, a species of literal mortification. And, following the Giant way, they will die of loneliness. "Singularly" so, believe me!

LOKI: One being? But I sensed a moment, several!, in which your minions seemed to rise against you.

U-L: Oh, we have our Biblical parallels. Mono-god created all yet that included Lucifer and his Angelic Third: old stories for Old Schnorri!

SCHNORRI(prelapses): Huh? What? [Lapses] Zzzzz....

LOKI: Yet and still.

U-L: No. You were thrust into a hall of mirrors, Demi-Deity, into Zeno's barbershop. My mind was distributed throughout the Throne Room. As to the rebellion you picked up on: one maybe at odds with himself, you know. No. What Giants offer our imaginers is not change, but a novel adaptation to the way they already are: captive to a static self-image, spinning back forever: a truly *solitary* confinement.

THOR (as if crashing a pity-party): ***STOP THE MUSIC!!*** Holy jumpin' Jesus! *None* of this makes sense to me. Inundating word-flow uninterrupted by meaning! And if it's someone's idea of a joke, I for one don't get it!! I feel like I'm straining at a gnat. Or that the truth balloons away from me, just when I think I have it cornered. Rather like...? Rather like my rasslin' match with your wet-nurse, Scammer.

UTGARD-LOKI: *Ach*, you had that one made-in-the-shade, Hambone, had you only known. You couldn't win, of course, but you couldn't lose, either.

THOR: Make it plain!

U-L: Madly! As I was just preminding your brighter brother, Giants don't age and neither do Deities.

THOR: What of it?

U-L: Well, my wet-nurse---Elli, your rasslin' partner?---: she was a humanoid representation of Old Age. You couldn't overcome what you had no need to. And she couldn't inflict her temporal woes upon a being who only exists from adventure to adventure. ...Until Roknarok, of course. Until the big dust-up before which our present encounter stands as a somewhat minor skirmish, a ramping, a sabre-rattling.

THOR: I will die in that dust-up. I know this.

U-L: As will I, Thor. In fact, in its last moments both sides will claim victory, a mutually-Pyrrhic affair. Closer to the facts would be the claim, made by some, that my side and yours died just in time for the humans to lose their faith in our physical presence.

LOKI: That they may believe in us in a different way.

U-L (with seeming regret): Just so. But not yet. Not yet. [Clashing piano music: late Scriabin and mid-period Monk; fades away] ...Oh, *you* will at least garner human sympathy. There will be none for the likes of me. Compassion for the Giants? ...I certainly can't count on Forrester for a proper view of our life-case: himself has little science and less math! And no character can count on his Reader to *take things further*, can he? We thought we'd evolved through self-selection. You Gods have witnessed the result: We have become ourselves. *My* self. All I possess is the power to delude; and I've used it to delude the deluder-of-deluders. When we take you on, come the great battle, we will win...to our minds. And you will win...to yours. Then we will both disappear, become legend. [Brightening up:] ...On the other hand, the legend defines the scale of the map, doesn't it? Meaning will out! Goodbye, my worthy opponents! See you by the near-silence of Nothing.

THOR (grabbing his hammer): I don't see why I can't just simplify matters!

(40)

The   pictorial   violence   of   the   ensuing   sequence requires/defies narration. Oh, there was undoubted dialogue, but it doubtless possessed the bland character of nearly all cinema coming out of Hollywood from the mid-60s onward, an as-yet unperioded period which---under the pretense of "realism" and re-telling "true stories"---placed an iron taboo on elevated language, poetry, and wit. It were more accurate to put it this way: chasing the buck, as usual, late-Modern Hollywood understood (as the blind worm does) that it would, soon enough, lose out to a technology that could actually *involve* its audience. Unable to muster that, it offered spectacular opportunities for viewer-identification. And that, in effect, levied a fatwa on any scripted lines the viewer, himorherself, wouldn't say, given the circumstances. ...The despair at the heart of this process is meant, here, as a commentary on Utgard-Loki's view of the human ego and his predicted consequences of its future enthronement.

All right, what went down?, you'll want to know.

(41)

'Twas simple: Thor restored himself by acting in character.

In his agon 'gainst one Giganticly-disguised tentacle of the Midgard Serpent---at once a flash-back 'n' a flash-forward---he'd taken a hit for the team and it had left him, briefly, a receptor rather than a broadcaster. Thor fell into this, having already surrendered his will in the drinking bout. And, after dropping Trouble's paw, he lost his plastic form in the rasslin' match. In all three trials, he was struggling for all of us, you know---for me, as well!---and it opened the Deity to the perspectives of others...which, with characteristic crudity, he made immediately his own. [My Reader may well marvel at this God's willingness to will away his will in furtherance of a story (his, yes, but ours as well); it renders him an authentic hero...in his Narrator's eyes, at least.] But this could never satisfy such a being, not for long. And when his new host of viewpoints failed to offer a coherent picture of the world around him, Thor reached for his hammer.

And all the words in the world might range against him but none there were (or are) that could hold Thursday's arm in check, once his mind was set. If he must dash out the brains of this Giant because the Deity found his rap maddeningly incomprehensible, if then this would seem a blow struck in ignorance, for the sake of ignorance, and productive of naught but ignorance...so be it. Thor had, in the end, wearied of not being wholly himself.

[He little recked, Reader, that his Narrator's one unmodified belief is that whole-hearted acts, even when patently destructive, always help others to see things more clearly, help them to get the point, even at times the joke. Why? Because they partake of necessity.]

And so our Leading Man took things into his own hands.

...Not that it worked. No, in fact, the slow-motion effect displaying the hammer-toss (more Hollywood, sorry) only rendered more bitter---for Thor and for all who'd identify with him---its crystalline futility: the viewer sees the weapon leave the God's hand, watches it turn end-over-end in space, e'er-so-slowly, unerringly heading for the massive brow of the Jint-of-Jints, only to witness the latter's sum-and-substance melt, thaw, and resolve itself into a dew just when the sweetness of contact seemed most inevitable, most desirable, most needed.

(42)

Yes, but there be no denying a God who has come back to himself. His hammer having returned to hand, Thor raged and raked through the wind-scattered pixils that constituted his former/future nemesis, eyes wild, arms a-flail.

"I'll lay waste to his city, to his entire tribe!" the God bellowed. "Let's settle this now! We'll *soon* see if they be 'one being' or a host of mediocre, self-imitating villains, after all. I'm curious to learn their true, un-shifted shapes! Perhaps the Big Galoot quivers hidden behind one of his proto-clone resemblers!!"

"Knock yourself out," chided Loki, pleased.

But Thor wasn't listening. Once again magnificently berserk, the Thunderer reached the gates of Utgard in five heroic strides; then, winding up like Christy Matthewson about to issue the screwball-of-screwballs, risking surgery it would take a Mediterranean Sun-God to heal, he let fly (left arm in pronounced pronation) that stone-skin-and-wood extension of himself, of his soul, sent it winging toward the unknown authors of his inevitable death.

(43)

Yes, yes, Utgard disappeared, as you knew it would. But, what's more, Thor's hammer disappeared as well....

For a seeming age, the God stood there, staring at a new-found nothingness, his pitching arm extended, its hand open; stood there—resolutely unknowable, even to me.

Loki stepped behind his brother, spoke into his left ear: "It will return.   The   Giants---multiform   or   Singular---have sequestered themselves in another time, remote from ours. Your hammer is seeking them there."

THOR(free, finally, to be Dramatic on his own):   Then it will find them!

LOKI: But the future is as various as the past, my Brother. In some versions it *will*, yes; and the obliteration of the tempting represented by these creatures will be celebrated as a great boon to humankind. In other telling, though, the Giants simply *move on* when e'er the hammer appeareth on their event-horizon. And   there   are   other   tales,   even-more-obscure,   more slippery,hard to make out on my mind-screen....   But your hammer always comes back to you: you wouldn't be yourself without it.

THOR (angrily): But in the one "telling" that seems to me the here-and-now? Where is my hammer **there**?

LOKI: Look in thy hand.

[The hammer appears there]

THOR (only somewhat placated): Yes. Hm. [Fondles his tool]

LOKI (aside, *sotto voce*, to the Narrator): One *detests* Magic Realism.

THOR: But did it do its job?, my hammer.

LOKI: Unknowable. Again, I say it: content is the mystery. We've **no** idea how this our tale will be received...if it be received at all! And the reception is the resolution.

THOR (turning his returned anger onto Loki): Whatever *that* means!! And in all these plausible futures---those my mind can conceive and those it cannot---, are you similarly slimy?, aloof?, "charming"?, treacherous??

LOKI (brightly riant): You sound like Athena, praising her beloved Ulysses: "So plausible, shrewd, and shifty"! Will I be all of that?, what you said? Well, more often than not, I suppose, because all that is in my nature. But I do not always follow my nature. And that is also in my nature.

THOR (grim; determined): So am I to hold on---maybe forever!---not knowing whether I have changed the ending or not? Not knowing whether the great battle I've heard about *all my life* will be a struggle against opponents of substance or of shadow? Or if the battle is already waged and won, my consciousness the proof of Aesirian victory? ...Or, indeed, if my undoubted unknowingness displays our profound defeat?

LOKI: That's the size of it. If humans cannot see beyond their own ends, how then can we?

THOR (with a Godly shrug): Well, it's clear to me that it's time to go back. I've much to think over, don't I?, during our long slog home. And I've an angle more attuned to incidence than to reflection, a sensibility---how did you put it, Loki?---better met with pounding than with pondering.

LOKI (sighs; speaking as to a child): Actually...there won't be any *going back*, Brother. You'll just... be there.

THOR: Huh?

THIALFI: One moment, Thor.

THOR: You address me by name, Boy?

THIALFI: Only because we're running out of time, Sir.

LOKI (harshly): "Time"?? As if you'd learned to take its measure while Thor and I were floundering. As if you'd "grown up" during this, my storied brother's journey, perhaps? As if this were all-about-you, all along, a forcedly Norse-y *Bildungsroman?* You've run and lost a rigged face, that's all, Kid. Minor character, no more than that.

ROSKVA: Hear him out.

LOKI: Oho! Another newly-emboldened voice breaks wind! Angels and ministers of grace defend us!!

THIALFI: It's just that I think you two are too hard on yourselves and on each other. [Two-beat pause] Loki, you would infect your brother with your half-Gigantic awareness of the last things. In fact, you cannot help but do so. You do this, I think, because you envy him his freedom.

LOKI: "Envy"?! Envy Thor? I? Karmic relief!

THIALFI: We wouldn't expect you to admit your one pure emotion. You are the past-master of life-displaced-from-life, of life displayed, of life-the-lie. And, somewhere deeply within, you understand the implications of this: that something is missing. Something you can't simply imitate or comment upon. Something in your brother that is forever beyond you.

LOKI: Name it!

THIALFI (artlessly): An unrehearsed freedom.

THOR: And just how am I "free"?

THIALFI: In that you recognize naught but what is necessary and act accordingly. Our local example?: you needed your curiosity satisfied---that's what lies at the root of this, your journey, does it not?---and it **is** satisfied because you have become yourself again. *As you were*, as it were: in the military sense. At ease. Angry. You are he who throws the hammer.

THOR: But I sought knowledge...and failed to find it.

THIALFI: You've told yourself that. Did it resonate? ...Nay, I think you sought, rather, a continuation of your own stellar being, through events that would only serve to extend your legend.

THOR: But this feels like my life, not my legend.

THIALFI: My point! Your freedom's a process not of learning but of involvement. You will emerge again in your next adventure.

THOR: How do you know this?, any of it? Horseshit.

[Thor turns away without waiting for an answer]

THIALFI (to Thor's back): I've just been paying attention, that's all. [To Loki:] And as to you, Trickster: I meant no potted calumny. Envy imitates: it is no answer but it is always a beginning: the word a comment on its object. Hence, the world is simply unimaginable without you.

LOKI: What "world" is that?

THIALFI: The human world, of course. Midgard. I speak to you as an ultimate inheritor, that is: as a mortal. We need the likes of both of you...although not in the same sense that you need us: it's not directly reciprocal.

ROSKVA: Hark unto my brother: the Real world belongs to those who would be buried in it. Immortality is evanescent. In terms of human need?: it flickers, it comes and goes.

LOKI: You, Girl, seem obnoxiously sure of yourself.

ROSKVA: Do I? If so, it's for one obvious---if hitherto overlooked---reason, Loki: I am the one character in this tallish, radial tale who may be blessed with **extension**, the only one among us who is capable...of reproduction.

LOKI: What?! Are you already with child? When did *that* happen?

[Thor turns turtle, faces Roskva]

THOR: Who's the daddy? [Indicates Loki] Either of us? Your own brother? That fucking Giant??

THIALFI: Is it I?

LOKI: Schnorri? Forrester?

ROSKVA: Chill, all of you. It has yet to happen. [Collective sigh from all about her] Yet it may! The ripeness is all. And if it proves necessary, then I shall be free to let it happen. [To Thor:] Thanks for that, Thursday! Perhaps it was for this, your one structural insight, that I saved you from terminal self-involvement? [Quietly, to all assembled:] No, you'll find no mention of this in Schnorri. [Finger to lips] Hush, don't awaken him. He's the Red King....

[Thor turns his back again; steps away]

(44)

LOKI (addressing Roskva sharply, spoiling the would-be didactic mood): Being merely "capable" of something seems a rather passive accomplishment.

ROSKVA: "Passive"? Hardly. Whatever must be I shall will into being. ...Catch up, Loki: we're not still *showing off* for your distant relatives.

LOKI: A "willed necessity"?, as with spontaneous generation? Inelegant. Unlikely.

ROSKVA: Impossible, rather.

LOKI: Well, yes.

ROSKVA: Then it's time we all remembered---at once!---that we dwell in the realm of myth, where, as outsize characters, it is our strict business to **impose**. And you, Loki, and your brother, and my brother and I, and Master Sturluson, and even our sometime Narrator: we will all remain in that realm. Only our Reader may leave at will. ...In fact, she's about to detach her consciousness. We must bid her goodbye! 'Tis only just: she's swung with us all the way.

LOKI: I assume you address the Reader as "she" out of some mythic priority of the female, or....

ROSKVA: No, because she is my opposite. That fifth impossibility you were looking for, earlier. [With a frank countenance:] Goodbye, Reader.

LOKI: Not so fast, human! You seem to be implying that this tale *represents* your baby. At least in Forrester's pagan retelling? A "virtual" reproduction: how bleeding contemporary! I wonder that you kept silent about it as long as you did!!

THIALFI: That's not what she's about, Lodestar. All my sister meant was this: nothing **stated** herein is possible; only our Reader escapes characterization. She is...unimaginable.

LOKI (changing his tone?, his tune?): Ah.... Ah.... Okay, I get it. Well, Kids, I've long known that you two would bring meaning to your being here. I just didn't savvy the how of it. Okay. ...But aren't we *all* forgetting something?

ROSKVA: I don't think so. My goodbye-to-the-Reader ought to have spelled the end. What's been forgotten? What?

THIALFI: Yeah, what?

LOKI: This!: we have left my bully brother behind, once again. He ought always to be in the forefront. In that respect, we prove no better than the soulless Giants!

[Roskva and Thialfi utter a noisy verbal-confusion, all about readers 'n' writers, being 'n' time, necessity 'n' the awareness of mortality, authority 'n' will, *usw.*]

LOKI: Okay, put a lid on it, both of you!! [Yawns] And listen up: I'd wager my anima---my very animus!--- that Thunderdunder here is far, far more important than any reader of these words, yes, more important even than Capital R, of whatever gender! Regard the God! [Thor stands in vibrant silence: inanimate, stolid, emotionally-disciplined] Regard him!: our recent speeches reach him not, make no sense to him.

ROSKVA: Nor should they. [Yawns herself]

THIALFI (yawning): No.

LOKI (wincing): How little you know!! But for my brother's strength, his good left arm, we'd all fall apart: face it, you two! And so...? And so, let us turn to *him* for the last word. [The humans share a speaking glance, suddenly unsure of themselves (or perhaps merely sharing in the general lassitude: cowed, canny, or about to conk out: I can't tell, tired myself!); Loki (with heartiness summoned from somewhere), appeals to his back-turned brother:] A song, Thor!; to carry us all off-stage, where sleep awaits! [To the Narrator:] Be there beds in the post-fictional Green Room?

[No narrative answer; Thor remains unmoved; the humans stare at Thor, yawn, remain silent; stasis threatens to stifle everything]

(45)

LOKI (with seeming humility, unwonted dignity, addressing yet again his brother's back): Thor, Old Man, I can't speak for the humans but I for one apologize for freezing you out...with our hightoned palaver about authority and myth, about the meaning of our context. We were but flittering, frittering, self-flattering.

THOR (slowly, ponderously turning to his 'tagonist): Ohhhhhhhh, that's all right, Loki. One cannot help but be himself, can he? In fact, I wasn't really listening, not really. Tripping on myself, I was. A more-engrossing subject.

LOKI: Now *that's* what I like to hear!

THOR: Oh, well, I *did* pick up on a **bit** of what you-all were beatin' your gums about, afore I tuned out.

LOKI: And?

THOR: And I hafta admit my mind has a devil of a time wrapping itself around the notion of the humans as *our* creators, Loki.

LOKI: Why?

THOR: Why? Because I feel so...indifferent towards them.

LOKI: But there's justice in that: they are indifferent towards us.   Ultimately.   ...They may be wooed---through the seductive promise of more perfect bodies---to Jotenheim and its imaginary Singularity.   If so, they are lost.   ...And I suspect that if our Narrator were not himself about to put paid to his final chapter, he'd dismiss the concept as a passing fancy.

THOR (uncomprehending?):   Why would anyone, even a human?, fancy becoming a Giant?

LOKI (sighs):   I know.   Your Giant is just a machine that knows he's a machine, that's all: all-one-being, solving the "problem" of community's self-limiting shelf-life;   strength through rigidity, nay, frigidity;   life reduced to information;   unimpeded by Time but, by the same token, ignorant of music.   [To the Reader:]   How about you?   Roll down that evolutionary river!   Would you rather be human reason aware-of-itself or a God like himself or me?   Or....   [Yawns; to Thor:]   Any more loose threads, Threadbare?

THOR: Well...are we really at the end, then?

LOKI: So it appears.   Time for this radio play to cut to a commercial...or for our networks to identify themselves.   ...Or, as our humans here would have it: time for the Reader to dis-attach her informed source---to pull out, to break off, to free herself from the likes of us.

THOR: Not sure I believe that *that's* what's happening.

LOKI: Nor I, Brother, not really.   Indeed, it smacks overmuch of an out-dated Humanism [To the Reader]:   a *capitalization* intended as a value-added identity-jest?

THOR: But if we **are**...at an ultimatum of sorts---and leaving aside the open question of your momentary sincerity, my

Betrayer---then, yes, I *should* like to sing a song.   [Yawns mightily; the others echo it]   ...And, oh yes, I feel I am losing consciousness, myself.   Fading into...a memory not my own?: that's an alien thought! So if I've a song in me, I'd best get it out, while I'm yet myself?

LOKI: Do.

[Loki and the humans form a clump on the ground; yawn & stretch]

THOR(singing):

I give my purpose not-a-lot-of thought, em-

brace necessity with all that I've got, and I

plead the Norns will someway indicate

how to begin-again-with-a true clean slate!

ROSKVA & THIALFI (singing, drowsily):

More! More! More!

LOKI (spoken, alertly): Less!

THOR (sung more slowly, haltingly as the humans fall to sleep and begin to snore):

More or less, I *get* that it's nearly time for bed, that I

only speak when my dialogue is read and my

life within this world lies at an end...'til a

future Reader let his disbelief...suspend!

[Spoken, rhetorically:] But it sure doesn't *feel* that way! Not to me.

LOKI: Amen, Brother! [To the Narrator:] I'm pleased to see the notated music yet again a laggard second-fiddle to its lyrics!

THOR (noting that the humans have dropped off): That wasn't meant to be a lullaby, you know.

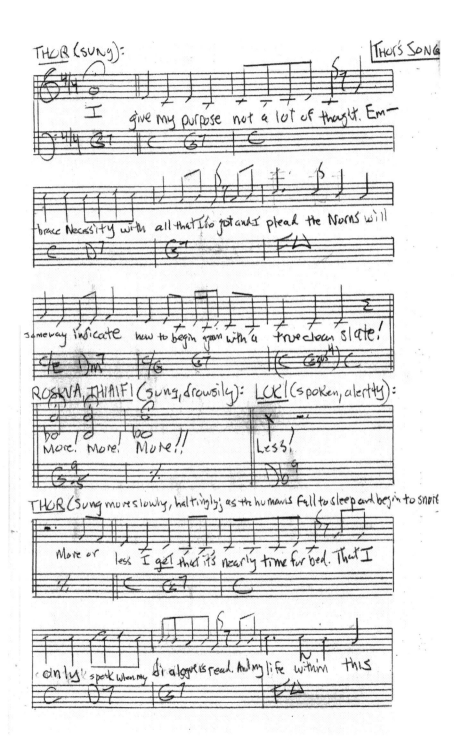

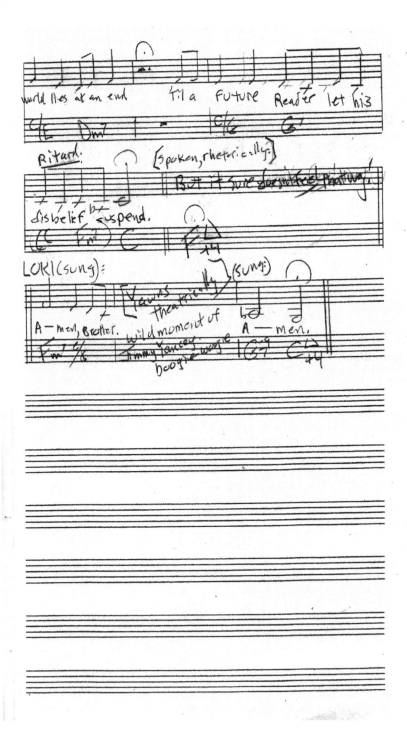

LOKI: It doesn't take much to lull them.

THOR: Sometimes it seems to me that all they get from us is our self-image, fortress 'n' mattress.

LOKI: But they're after more than that, Thor. Grandeur is not in the human skill-set, so they must seek it elsewhere, imagine it. [Re-yawns] Oh, they may yet find their way out, find their way into something different, less...repetitive.

THOR: These two?

LOKI: Their *kind!*, my sweet, dim, beloved Brother, who never met a generalization he wouldn't labor to particularize...and is none the worse for that! [*Mild und leise:*] Yes, as one of the creatures in their reflexive bestiary, I'd like to believe that humans may, *through necessity* [Tips an imaginary hat to Thor], come to change their ways. And it may well be through an internal discovery, there, all the time, waiting to be known. But it won't be through the likes of us, Thor. Not through us. Even ol' Schnorrer knew that Jesus was a nobler construction than either you or me. And look, if you've the stomach for it, at all that was done in *his* name. No. We who are imaginary: we cannot really help. An "empowered imagination"---*pace* the Sainted Sixties---will *not* save the species: it is not a sufficient condition for change. [Happier:] Of course, what it *might* do is cause the humans to fashion *new* Gods. Hey, Thor, we might find ourselves re-configured, re-jiggered! [Re-re-yawns] Oh, well, none of this should have seemed exotic to me: I'm certain I've been here, before. Giants? After all, I have coupled with a full-blooded female Giant...who will, after my final betrayal, come to my aid. But, perhaps, I too only remember myself *as I go along...*

THOR (charmed by Loki's voice): ...Sorry, couldn't follow yer train of thought, Brother. Doesn't matter. *I am that I am.* ...Did I say that wrong?

LOKI (with finality): No! [Yawns, also with finality] I'm losing it, Thor. You, too, by the looks of ya. But remember, Brother: you outright *love* to dream, so ENJOY YOURSELF! Catch you at the Round-up, if not before. Me, I've got *worlds* to betray!! [Nods off, only to wake up elsewhere]

THOR: Ah, well.

[The God essays the hugest yawn of all and joins the others in their clump.

[Soon all are snoring 'n' snorting in concert; the effect may be randomly rhythmical for comic purposes, but don't belabor it.

[The Narrator invites his Reader to join himself and the actors/characters in the temporary salvation of a deep snooze. Yes?]

SCHNORRI (revealed: recumbent, becrowned, high above the stage, swathed in a scarlet robe): *Zzz. Zzz. Zzz....*

[General snoring continues during the postlude and even after, as the audience files out, puzzling many, delighting a few. Questions flutter through the air: "Can a God actually change?", "Can a stone right-winger undergo a Pauline switcheroo?", "And put his soul on the line for a universal community foreshadowed by The People?", "Desiring Reality over dreams?", "The flood of others over the dam of the self?": oh, well, all one question, really. One audient at a time. You.

[The Hammerer has returned to himself; Loki, to an unknown elsewhere; our two humans, to memory; the bard, to an uncollective consciousness; and I, to silence. Where would you go?]

JULY 2016
NEW YORK

THOR'S THEME (Postlude)

79591795R00065

Made in the USA
Columbia, SC
05 November 2017